HER BURIED SECRET

A ROSEMARY RUN THRILLER

KELLY UTT

2020 Standards of Starlight Paperback Edition

www.standardsofstarlight.com

ISBN: 978-1-952893-01-8

Cover art by Elizabeth Mackey

PROLOGUE

Penelope Cline had always known she wasn't good at telling lies. Or, for that matter, keeping secrets. Her friends knew it, too, which is why they rarely asked her to keep anything in confidence.

As a kid, Penelope had held her breath every time she tried to tell a fib. It was comical, really. Her parents could gauge the truthfulness of their daughter's statements by watching her breath for a minute or two. When she was lying, Penelope would purse her lips and inhale big gulps, as if she was sipping air through a straw. Then she'd exhale in loud, dramatic bursts once she couldn't hold it in anymore.

Like Pinocchio, whose nose grew when he wasn't truthful, Penelope's body told everyone around her when something wasn't right.

One time, at nine-years-old, Penelope had entered a bank to deposit some allowance into her savings account, but had made a carefully calculated withdrawal instead.

Her mother had waited in the car, initially oblivious to her daughter's plan.

"Is your mom or dad with you today?" Bernice Tenpenny, the stern old lady behind the counter, had asked.

Bernice had probably been amused to see the withdrawal slip filled out in the amount of eighty-seven dollars. Not a round or even number, like one would expect. And in a child's handwriting, no less.

"My mom is outside waiting in the car," Penelope had replied, twirling a strand of long brown hair around one finger.

"Does she know you're making a withdrawal?"

"Yes, ma'am," Penelope had answered, sipping air.

Bernice had looked at her skeptically, so Penelope expounded. "My baby brother is sleeping in his car seat and Mom didn't want to wake him. She told me to go ahead by myself and explain what I was here to do."

Penelope had been precocious for nine. And smart as a whip. She'd had her reasons for the withdrawal from her savings account. But she was still a child, after all. She hadn't yet developed the judgment of an adult.

There had been a few moments of silence as Bernice sized the girl up and considered whether to honor her withdrawal request. Every second had been excruciating for Penelope as she stood, cautiously waiting. She had nearly cracked under the pressure, but instead she had focused on how funny it was that a bank teller had the last name Tenpenny. She could easily read and pronounce the moniker that was printed neatly on the woman's name tag.

She wondered if Bernice had chosen her job at the bank because of her name.

What a hoot, Penelope thought as she smiled sweetly and put a casual hand over her mouth to disguise the sips of air. She had hoped Bernice could see her smiling by looking at her cheeks and eyes. It had been hard to smile with pursed lips. But Penelope had held steady. She had felt like an actress giving the performance of her life.

To find the fortitude to continue her act as the minutes ticked by, Penelope had shifted her thoughts to the reason she was at the bank in the first place.

It was about a tent, of all things.

There had been a green camping tent that had caught Penelope's eye when she'd seen it pictured in a glossy Sears Wishbook. She had envisioned herself reading and playing in the tent in her family's fenced backyard. She had thought, if she was lucky, it could provide a place of peace and refuge. She needed such a place. Desperately.

Most kids would have simply asked their parents to order a tent for them. But not Penelope. She knew her mom would say no.

Money had been tight for the family ever since her dad had been laid off from his job the year prior. They'd exhausted their savings, and Jean Cline, Penelope's stay-at-home mom, wasn't handling the stress well. Jean had even seemed jealous of the five dollar allowance that Felix Cline, Penelope's dad, left on the top of the girl's dresser each week.

To get the tent, Penelope had been forced to hatch an elaborate plan. She didn't have a debit or credit card, or know how mail or phone orders worked. So, she had done the only thing she could.

Enter the Sunnyday Sales Club, a fundraising partner for Penelope's elementary school. Kids who sold enough of the club's stationary and gifts could choose from prizes, one of which was a spacious green tent, just like the one in the Sears catalog. When Penelope saw it, she immediately knew what she had to do.

She'd sell enough to get the tent. Easy peasy.

The plan had seemed foolproof until Penelope's door-to-door efforts failed to produce the required sales volume. It was at that point the savings account and the bank withdrawal had come into play as the girl had needed the eighty-seven dollars to buy enough stationary and gifts to qualify for the tent as a prize. Penelope told herself she'd worry about how to hide the surplus products when they arrived.

One step at a time. One lie at a time.

Sip... Sip... And hold.

It had been a roundabout way of getting what she wanted. But one had to admire Penelope's tenacity and resourcefulness.

At the bank, against all odds, Bernice had cooperated. The old lady had chuckled as she dispensed the cash into Penelope's hand and counted out loud, right up to eighty-seven. Penelope had thanked Bernice, then did her best calm-walk out of the building, completing the first act of the performance of her life. Or so she thought.

Penelope had stuffed the cash deep into her pants pockets so Jean wouldn't see, then climbed into the backseat of the family's big black car as if nothing out of the ordinary had happened.

Jean had noticed that her daughter seemed to be holding her breath, but decided to watch quietly, perhaps planning to discuss it another time. Jean couldn't imagine what Penelope would have lied about while inside the bank. She had been just nine-years-old.

Little did Jean know what the girl was up to.

And little did young Penelope know how much the Sunnyday Sales Club experience from her childhood would mirror the most dramatic turn of events in her adult life, each complete with numerous occasions to awkwardly hold her breath.

Thirty-something Penelope and her three closest girlfriends shared a secret.

A woman was dead. She had disappeared under mysterious circumstances at a party the friends had attended together, and they knew much more than was reported to the authorities.

1

"I'm a good person, you know," Penelope proclaimed.

She was seated cross-legged on the wide dock behind Marshall Erving's house, her halter-top party dress billowed out around her. The vintage boho vibe of the floral-print dress paired well with Penelope's long, side-swept braid. She was the picture of sweet innocence as she fiddled nervously with her silver bracelet. The silky waters of Sweet Balm Bay lapped rhythmically against the steel support beams below. She was less than half an hour from home in Rosemary Run, but it felt like a world away.

Spring was in the air. Birds chirped eagerly as newly bloomed seaside daisies clung to bluffs along the banks of the bay. The smell of freshly cut grass hung in the air, still potent from mowers who had tended to Marshall's property the prior afternoon. It was a perfect morning. Mother Nature was, apparently, unaware of the distress Penelope was experiencing.

Marshall and his husband, Reginald Johns, had thrown the big, booming party the night before. It had been a grand affair with decadent food and luxurious trimmings, but neither homeowner was anywhere to be found as the sun came up and shone on a new day. Penelope figured the police probably had them at the station, asking questions and taking official statements.

That's where she thought Marshall and Reggie should be, anyway. Wasn't that the way it usually worked on television?

Seated next to Penelope in a red Adirondack chair was her oldest friend, Cheryl Edwards. Cheryl kicked one leg nervously, her body draped sideways across the wooden planks as her curve-hugging pink dress and coordinating pale pink nail polish played against her bleach-blonde hair. The asymmetrical ruffles along the hemline of Cheryl's dress danced in the gentle breeze as she kicked. Penelope had always thought Cheryl looked like a pin-up model. She certainly had the hourglass figure for it.

"We know you are," Cheryl said. Her voice was shaky, but not shaky enough, as far as Penelope was concerned.

"Of course, you're a good person," Hana Kim added from the other side of Cheryl. "We shouldn't have to tell you that."

She, too, was on a red Adirondack chair, only she sat up straight and tall. Hana hugged her knees tight against her chest, her off-the-shoulder black dress pulled taut. She seemed quieter than usual, and not just because it was early in the morning. Penelope thought Hana's jet-black hair and olive skin made her look exotic. She was the most glamorous of the bunch. And that was saying something. Even under the stress of their situation, Hana had the air of a glitzy runway model.

Meg Harris rounded out the foursome. She was splayed out face down on the deck just beyond Hana's chair, her thick, blonde, curly hair disheveled. Black mascara was smeared under her eyes. Meg had imbibed far too many glasses of wine the night before, and she wasn't holding her alcohol well. She was out of it, groggy and disconnected, yet she still looked beautiful. She wore a rose-colored, backless dress made of lace and featuring a thick ribbon that tied artfully around her waist. Only the ribbon was out of place now, a visual reminder of what had happened.

Penelope knew she was pretty in a down-to-earth, natural sort of way. She could put on a party dress and clean up nicely. Yet her friends were on another level. She often felt like the ugly duckling among world-class beauties.

It was no wonder, really. Jean had always been ashamed of her own physical appearance for reasons Penelope never quite understood, and she had passed her insecurities down to her unwitting daughter. Though the effects had been tempered by Felix's kind encouragement and good parenting, Penelope had taken on too much of Jean's low self esteem as her own. She had carried it, even when it wasn't hers.

As Penelope sat fretting about what they had seen the night before, she was, perhaps, more aware of what she lacked than ever. If things went like usual, she knew her attractive friends would steer clear of trouble more easily than she would. It was a sad, but true fact of life: Extraordinarily beautiful women had it made. Life was easier for them. People bent over backwards to forgive their transgressions and to do them favors. The same wasn't necessarily true for average-looking women like Penelope.

"Just stop," Meg said as she rubbed her temples, curls bobbing. "Nobody is questioning your character, Pen."

"It feels like they're going to," Penelope replied. "It's only a matter of time."

This was the way it always was with Cheryl, Hana, and Meg. Penelope worried while they skated through life effortlessly. At least, that's how it had seemed.

"Not true, Pen," Hana said, shifting her weight in the chair as she hugged her knees tighter. "I'm with Meg on this one. No one is questioning your character. You're getting worked up when, most likely, that's an overreaction."

Of course, Hana was with Meg. She was always with Meg.

"What?" Penelope asked. "Are you seriously suggesting that I'm overreacting right now? Because I don't think I am. This is serious."

Hana shot Cheryl a knowing glance, which was then shared with Meg. They were deciding how to handle Penelope. They didn't believe there was anything to be too concerned about.

"We know," Cheryl said.

Cheryl was the one most likely to try to appease Penelope, when and if it had to be done.

But this was different. Penelope thought so, anyway.

"Maybe we should talk about what we saw last night," Penelope suggested.

"What good will that do?" Hana asked.

Hana preferred to sweep things under the rug whenever possible, and she was a master at doing so. Her parents had been the same way. Hana had claimed it was typical of her Asian upbringing and that she came by it honestly, but Penelope wasn't so sure that was all there was to it. Penelope often thought it was just an excuse to get out of the hard stuff in life. She had discussed Hana's avoidance behaviors with Cheryl, who had agreed. Sometimes, facing up to life's difficulties was necessary. No one said it had to be pleasant.

"Really?" Penelope asked, incredulous. "This again, Hana?"

"Shh," Cheryl purred, leaning sideways and placing a hand over Penelope's mouth.

It was a silly gesture, as if the two of them were back in grade school with little more to worry about than where they'd end up in that day's lunch line.

Penelope's blood boiled as she flung her friend away. "Did you just shush me?" she asked.

Cheryl rolled her eyes and turned back to face Hana and Meg.

"Please, keep your voices down," Meg pleaded. "Can't a girl have a hangover in peace?"

Penelope exhaled loudly, buzzing her lips. "Incredible," she muttered.

"What's that supposed to mean?" Hana asked, her lip twitching like it did when she was irritated.

"What do you think it means?" Penelope replied. "I think the response here is incredible. You're incredible… only *NOT*."

Cheryl straightened herself in the chair and raised a

hand in the air between Penelope and Hana as if she were a referee ready to break up a fight. "Ladies, please…"

Penelope knew it wasn't a time for foolishness or bickering. She was experienced in such matters. Although, her friends had no idea of the things her history held. Not even Cheryl knew what Penelope had been through.

"Look," Penelope began again, raising her voice. "I can't stress enough how serious this situation is. I don't know what you three witnessed last night, but I know what I saw. It wasn't pretty."

Penelope was wise enough to know that what they had seen made them liabilities. In fact, the guilty parties might soon be looking to cover their tracks. It was time to compare notes and get on the same page.

There might not be another opportunity.

"What, Pen?" Meg asked, exasperated. "Should we call in a priest and sit for confession?"

Hana chuckled. "Ooh, I know! We could put him on one side of the wooden fence at the edge of the property. Then we could glance at him ashamedly through the cracks."

Cheryl chimed in, "And we could have him position himself strategically so that everything from the nose down would be hidden. Like Wilson on that old TV show. *Home Improvement*, right?"

Everyone except Penelope laughed heartily at the thought. She, on the other hand, stood and let her hands rest on her hips.

"It's time we get it all out in the open between us," she urged.

Hana smirked. "Come on, Pen. Whatever is meant to be will work out. You know my prerogative."

Penelope's brows furrowed, and she lowered her voice as she spoke sternly to her friends. Someone had to be the heavy. The responsible adult. The voice of reason.

"Out with it," Penelope demanded. "*Right now.* I won't take no for an answer."

2

"Fine," Cheryl reluctantly agreed, gesturing towards Hana and Meg. "Let's humor her. Pen wants us to talk about what we saw here last night, so let's do that. She won't get off of our backs until we do."

"Finally!" Penelope exclaimed. "Thank you, Cheryl."

"You really should have been a school teacher," Cheryl said. "Kindergarten. Maybe first grade."

Penelope winked in her friend's direction. She knew she could be bossy. Sometimes, bossy was good.

"Okay, okay," Hana said. "But make it quick. I have places to be."

"Where do you have to be this morning?" Penelope asked. "You told me last night that you were planning a lazy morning at home."

"Plans change," Hana quipped. "And I'm not at home, if you haven't noticed, Ms. Bossypants. Just get on with it." She tossed her hair over one shoulder as she scowled.

"Meg?" Cheryl prompted. "Are you in?"

Meg was dozing off, in and out of consciousness. She

needed sleep. But now wasn't the time to get it. "What?" she asked, raising her head a few inches off the decking. "Are you talking to me?"

Hana leaned over and whispered into Meg's ear, apparently filling her in. A few digs at Penelope were, no doubt, included.

"Whatever," Meg mumbled, then began the slow process of getting herself into a sitting position. Her limbs were heavy, her mind still dulled by the effects of alcohol. Oddly enough, not a single blonde ringlet looked out of place. Her perfect hair was a stark contrast to her smeared and swollen face.

"Good," Penelope said, clasping her hands together as if she actually was in front of a classroom of young children. Cheryl had been right about that.

Penelope often wished she didn't have to be the steady voice of reason. It reminded her too much of her childhood. But someone had to do it. And sadly, no one else volunteered.

"I'll go first," Cheryl offered.

"Yes, great!" Penelope replied, excited. "It's just the four of us out here. Speak freely. Tell us everything. It's the best chance we have of making it through this."

"Okay," Cheryl continued. "I'll just say her name so it isn't the elephant: Audrey Ward. She's missing."

"And presumed dead," Hana added.

Penelope's eyes opened wide. She hadn't expected her friends to be so blunt, even though she had requested their honesty. "Wow," she breathed.

"Yeah, presumed dead," Meg confirmed. "How could she *not* be?"

"I don't know," Penelope replied. "She might have been alive when she was pulled out of the water. I couldn't tell."

"Now *that's* wishful thinking," Hana said, fiddling with a fingernail. "I saw her at the bottom of the pool. She looked lifeless."

"Cheryl," Penelope redirected, not wanting to talk about the most gruesome part just yet. "Let's get back to you. What did you see?"

Cheryl shrugged a shoulder, her pink dress shimmering in the sunlight as it moved. "I mean, I was with her earlier in the evening."

"Audrey?"

"Yeah, you know. I was showing her around. Showing her the ropes."

"Was it her first party?" Meg asked, squinting against the morning sun.

"First party with the group," Cheryl confirmed. "So, I tried to make her feel comfortable. Marshall and Reggie were busy entertaining more than just Audrey. I wanted to help out."

Penelope nodded. "Go on."

"I got her a drink to help her loosen up," Cheryl explained. "She asked the bartender for a strawberry daiquiri, which was cute. You could tell she was young. Inexperienced. She might as well have asked for a wine spritzer."

Meg found this especially funny and laughed out loud. Maybe she was still buzzed. It wasn't that funny. Penelope knew how it felt to be young and inexperienced. She wouldn't laugh at Audrey's expense.

"The bartender ended up making her something with pineapple and vodka," Cheryl continued. "He told her it would taste like pineapple upside down cake. It worked. She liked it. I pray she was at least twenty-one."

"Oh," Penelope mused. "I didn't even think about that. Let's hope we weren't serving alcohol to someone underage. That's the last thing we need right now."

"We?" Meg asked. "How did this become *we*?"

"Agreed," Hana added. "Marshall and Reggie own this house. Audrey's death should be on them. Not on us."

Penelope was growing frustrated with her friends. Especially Hana. She could be so callous and insensitive at the worst possible times.

"I'm just saying," Penelope continued. "We, in the collective sense, have plenty to worry about. And don't pretend you don't know what I mean. We can't leave all of this on Marshall and Reggie. We each have our own roles to play."

"Oh, we can and we will leave this on Marshall and Reggie," Hana reiterated. "I'm not getting mixed up in a murder investigation."

"We don't know that it's a murder investigation, do we?" Meg asked.

"Yeah, I heard the term disappearance," Cheryl confirmed. "Missing person. Nothing about murder yet."

"I don't even understand what happened, or how it happened," Penelope pondered. "But I want to." She stared out at the bay as she thought, a light wind dancing around her braid.

"So," Cheryl continued, moving right along. She seemed determined to get her side of the story out now that she had started. "There was a guy… a handsome devil… who was making eyes at Audrey. He was in his late twenties or early thirties. He had rich brown hair combed loosely off of his ears. He was muscular. And his smile… Man, oh, man. He had a smile that would surely make any woman melt. Kind of like Bradley Cooper."

Cheryl was infatuated with Bradley Cooper. She had seen every one of his movies. Some several times. Her favorite was *Silver Linings Playbook*, a point she took pride in because most people seemed to prefer *The Hangover*. Cheryl claimed to appreciate Bradley's more complicated and emotional side. Heaven knows what she'd do if she ever came face to face with him in person.

"Bradley Cooper?" Meg asked sarcastically. "Don't you say that about everyone?"

"Only the guys who actually look like Bradley Cooper," Cheryl replied. She stuck her tongue out at Meg, teasing.

"I'd do Bradley Cooper," Hana blurted.

"Same. Or any man who looks like him," Cheryl added.

The two of them clasped hands in a knowing high five as they smiled at each other.

"Right," Penelope confirmed. She really wished Hana would focus. And stop acting like such an ass.

"And?" Meg asked.

"And nothing," Cheryl replied. "That's about all I've got. I don't know if Cooper Clone ever approached Audrey. Or if they hooked up."

"You assume they hooked up?" Penelope asked.

"You assume they didn't?" Cheryl quickly replied. "That *is* what people do at these parties, Pen."

Penelope bristled. Her friends were not only more beautiful than she was, but also more comfortable with their sexuality. It wasn't that Penelope was uncomfortable, exactly. More like she'd had to be serious and hadn't had time for their type of antics. It had been that way for as long as she could remember.

As young kids, Penelope wasn't carefree like Cheryl because she'd had to watch over Jean. Being saddled with a mother like Jean had been a burden. Emotionally, Penelope had been the adult who cared for her mother when her dad was away. Felix knew Jean had issues, but Penelope often wondered if he'd realized the extent of them and the effect they'd had on her as a child. After Zach was born, Penelope had watched over him, too.

Cheryl's family was normal by comparison.

When Hana and Meg came into the picture during high school, Penelope had been hard at work figuring out how she would make it on her own in the world. She'd had no choice. While Hana, Meg, and Cheryl were out with boys and sleeping in late, Penelope was working two restaurant jobs to put gas in her old, beaten-up car and food in her belly. Not to mention, she was trying to keep up with her studies so she could get a scholarship for college. She didn't have parents who could pay tuition like the others did.

That's not to say that Penelope hadn't dated or become sexually experienced. She had. But everything she had done was in a more serious light. Boyfriends had been chosen carefully. Sex had been handled responsibly, almost always as part of a long-term relationship.

Sometimes, Penelope couldn't put her finger on what she was missing, or missing out on. But she felt it. The differences between Penelope and her friends remained palpable, just under the surface. There was an invisible barrier between them that Penelope knew she'd never be able to cross. Maybe she didn't want to.

What Penelope did want, was to one day lay down all the extra responsibility and breathe more easily. Maybe it was no wonder that she held her breath when she lied. The invisible, emotional weight she carried was heavy, literally taking her breath away. Maybe it was no wonder that she sought to hold on to that breath, carefully rationing it when she felt like she had to lie. She'd never really wanted to lie in the first place. She wanted to be seen as the good person she knew deep down that she was, even though her mother had made her think otherwise. Even as a grown woman, the battle raged inside of her.

"I know," Penelope replied to Cheryl. "Of course, I know."

"Sure you do," Hana jabbed. "Penelope Cline, the sex goddess…"

Meg chuckled.

"Come on, now," Cheryl said. "Let it be, Hana… Easy."

"Oh, I wouldn't say she's easy…" Hana continued, oblivious to Penelope's hurt feelings. "I'm afraid she's the opposite. I hear those legs are like Fort Knox. Maybe we should start calling her coochie The Vault."

All three of them laughed. They couldn't seem to help

themselves. Tears formed in Penelope's eye as she turned her back to her friends, the waters of the bay providing her comfort. She wondered if she should even call them friends, really. She hated feeling misunderstood.

"Don't turn away, Pen," Cheryl said. "Hana is just playing around. She doesn't mean anything by it."

Penelope held firm, wiping tears that rolled down her cheeks. She didn't want them to see her cry. That would only add to the humiliation. Silence fell over the dock as the moment became awkward and no one knew quite what to do. Birds continued their songs and the water continued to lap gently, but no one spoke.

Suddenly, Penelope felt two delicate hands on her shoulders. She could tell instantly that it was Hana.

"You're being such a downer, you might as well go lower. Into the water with you!" Hana said.

With a strong push and a kick, Hana sent Penelope toppling into Sweet Balm Bay.

The disbelief kept Penelope from fully realizing what was happening until she hit the cold water, her dress probably ruined. As the icy sensation shot through her, she wasn't sure whether the pains in her body were from embarrassment and emotional hurt or the temperature of the water itself. Either way, she convulsed in agony. But she didn't make a sound.

Penelope had learned long ago to keep her suffering quiet. She could still hear Jean's voice in her ear saying that no one liked a negative nelly.

3

_____

"Hana!" Marshall exclaimed. Penelope couldn't see him, but she heard his deep, booming voice coming down over the hill. "What are you doing? That was uncalled for. The water is chilly. It's colder than it looks."

At least someone was defending Penelope. Because she sure felt like she was being bullied by her so-called friends. Maybe they weren't really friends at all.

Marshall's footsteps quickened as he ran towards the dock and the bay. He moved fast. The last thing he wanted was another incident on his hands. But it was about more than that. Unlike Hana, Marshall cared for Penelope. He never would have pushed her into the water like that. Not without her permission. What Hana did had been plain mean.

"What?" Hana asked. "I was just playing around."

Penelope gulped as she treaded water and endeavored to keep her head above the surface. She was a strong swimmer, but these waters were deep. And the cold continued to overwhelm her. As she caught a glimpse of Hana on the dock above, Penelope thought she saw the woman smile. Hana looked like an evil villain. She appeared pleased with Penelope's struggle.

"Marshall!" Penelope managed, shifting her attention away from Hana and lifting one arm out of the water to signal him. "Help! I'm not doing well here."

Penelope could still talk. She wasn't drowning. But she was humiliated. She hoped her friends would leave and get out of her sight. She no longer cared to discuss what they had seen at the party.

"Hang on," Marshall said. "I'm coming."

Marshall was unusually tall at 6'5", and he was strong. He lifted weights and kept himself in tip-top physical condition. Plus, he was brave and selfless. He had been a volunteer firefighter in Rosemary Run before he married Reggie and moved into this mansion on the bay. Penelope was certain he'd help her.

"Get me," she pleaded. "It's cold. And I'm embarrassed."

Just as Penelope had expected, Marshall slung his shoes off and bounded into the water, then swam towards her. He was still wearing his tux from the party the night before, minus the coat and tie. He reached Penelope after a few long, smooth strokes. He positioned himself behind her and wrapped one muscular arm around her trim waist.

Marshall seemed forlorn. He was probably stressed about Audrey's disappearance. Penelope reevaluated her situation and thought she might have better luck talking to Marshall privately, without involvement from Cheryl,

Hana, or Meg. He seemed to share Penelope's level of concern. She was grateful that somebody did.

Penelope let her body relax and Marshall toted her to shore. It felt good to be up against him. He felt familiar.

"Thanks for this, my dear," Penelope whispered in Marshall's ear as he placed her on solid ground.

"I'll always save you," he replied, quietly so the others didn't hear.

Penelope and Marshall had a history. If Reggie hadn't come into the picture when he did, it might have been Penelope married to Marshall right now. It was a sore topic between the two of them. They both had regrets.

"My hero," Penelope added as she found her footing on the sand at the edge of the yard. Both shoes had toppled off into the bay. That fact pissed her off, but not as much as it should have.

"Too bad we couldn't save your shoes," Marshall added. "Were they expensive?"

"Not terribly," Penelope replied. "They weren't Jimmy Choos or anything."

Out of the corner of Penelope's eye, she saw Cheryl and Meg climbing down from the deck and heading towards her.

"Don't!" Penelope shouted. "Just go. Please."

"But we didn't…" Meg began.

Penelope put a palm up to stop her. "Leave it."

"Pen?" Cheryl tried, making her eyes like a puppy dog's. "I don't want to leave you like this."

Penelope shook her head in disbelief. It was too little, too late.

"I've got her," Marshall inserted. "Do as she asks and go. We'll call you later."

Penelope liked knowing that Marshall would look after her.

He was quite a catch. Dark hair, brooding blue eyes, and a kindness matched only by his physical strength. He sometimes reminded Penelope of her father. But there was more to it. She could actually see herself ending up with someone like Marshall.

Scratch that.

Penelope could see herself ending up *with Marshall*. Truth be told, she resented Reggie and the fancy lifestyle that had apparently drawn Marshall in. Penelope wanted a simple life. A kid or two. Maybe a couple of dogs. A little house with a big yard. She didn't need a mansion on the bay, and she knew Marshall could be happy without one. If only things could be different.

"Okay, we'll go," Cheryl said, backing away slowly.

"Call us, please," Meg added.

"At some point, sure," Penelope replied.

Hana was nowhere to be seen. She had apparently already made her exit.

Once the ladies were gone, Marshall and Penelope climbed onto the dock and took their seats in the Adirondack chairs. Penelope spread her dress out as far as it would go on either side, hoping the sun would help it dry out before she had to drive home. She didn't want her car soaking wet too.

"That wasn't how I expected to spend my morning," Penelope said, wiping her wet hair back away from her face. Her braid was gnarled and falling apart now.

"Me neither," Marshall added, rolling his pant legs up and wringing water out one section at a time. "Those bitches aren't good to you, Pen. Why do you keep hanging out with them?"

Penelope leaned her head against the wooden slats of the chair, soaking up the sun. "They're not all bad."

"Let me guess," Marshall tried. "You're going to tell me they're just misunderstood."

Penelope smiled. She was already in a much better mood. "I might have said something along those lines before. Maybe you've heard?"

Marshall smiled, too. There was an ease between them. "Once or twice."

He stretched one arm out, palm up, on the arm of his chair. It was an invitation. Penelope knew exactly what the gesture meant. The two of them had been through the same routine a million times. She met his hand, lacing her fingers through his.

"Oh, my dear, Marshall," she began. "Why is it that everything seems easier when we're together?"

He chuckled. "Huh. I hadn't thought about it in those terms. But you're right." He used one thumb to stroke the top of her hand. "Loving you is easy."

"Too bad you had to go and marry someone else," Penelope added, smiling coyly.

"Why? Would we have ended up together if I hadn't?"

Penelope knew the answer to that. Yes, they would have ended up together. Marshall had expressed his interest in her long before he'd even met Reggie. Penelope had been too insecure to reciprocate. Deep down, she didn't believe she deserved true love, so she had pushed it away. Again and again.

She hesitated before answering.

Even now, as she sat on the property Reggie owned, Penelope wanted nothing more than to profess her love for Marshall and ask him to leave his husband. In her dream world, Marshall would get his marriage annulled and tell Reggie he never really loved him. Not like he loved Penelope, anyway. Then the true lovebirds could settle down in Rosemary Run together.

Penelope had enough cash stashed away for a down payment on a little house in the country. And she had their lives together all planned out, right down to the paint colors and the breed of puppies they'd get. For the record, the exterior of the house would be a color called Honest Blue by Sherwin-Williams. It would pair well with smooth white hydrangeas in the flower beds out front and a wooden front door. The puppies would be medium-size mutts rescued from the local pound. Hopefully, at least one of the pups would be some sort of shepherd mix that would keep the kids rounded up when it was time.

"I'd like to think so," she said tentatively.

"What?" Marshall said, sitting up straight in his chair, a look of shock on his face. "Are you serious? You and me? Together?"

Penelope tightened her grip on his hand, tucking her lean fingers into his. She was tall for a woman at 5'11". No man had ever seemed like such a perfect fit. She could imagine their kids.

"What are you thinking about?" Marshall asked when

she didn't respond. "I can see the wheels turning in that pretty head of yours."

"It's silly."

"Whatever. You can tell me."

She sighed, not sure what she was even doing. "Um, thinking about our kids. They'd be tall."

"Our kids?!" Marshall asked in disbelief.

He had the look of someone completely exasperated. The look of someone who once envisioned the same thing, but had moved on. The look of someone reevaluating his entire life.

"Basketball players," Penelope added. "They'd have to be. Everyone who met them would instantly think basketball. It would be a shame if they didn't play. A waste, even."

"Okay, yeah," Marshall agreed. "They'd be tall, alright. But Pen, where is this coming from? I thought…"

Something about the situation with Audrey was making Penelope feel like she had nothing to lose. Women went missing all the time. Their lives ended all the time. Every hour of every day, it was happening somewhere. Not to mention, the things that she was doing… With her friends, for Reggie… At these parties… It wasn't her. Not really. Instead, she should be at home in the little blue house with Marshall. They didn't need all of this.

Penelope scolded herself for letting her life get this far out of hand.

"You thought wrong," she said simply. "You thought… Wrong."

Marshall lowered his brow as a look of confusion spread across his face. "Pen…"

"I know," she said. Then she threw caution to the wind, hoisted herself across the arms of the chairs, and kissed him on the lips.

Marshall's eyes nearly popped out of his head. Penelope could see his expression clearly, since they were joined at the lips and her eyes were still open as well. She didn't back away. After an awkward few seconds passed, Marshall relaxed into her, meeting her affection with his own.

4

"What was that for?" Marshall asked when Penelope finally pulled away.

"I don't know," she replied. "I just wanted to do it, so I did."

Marshall shoved a hand through his thick hair as he tried to comprehend. In the seat beside him, Penelope smiled. She couldn't remember the last time she'd felt so free.

"Hey," Marshall said, pulling his hand away. "What do you say we get back in the water? We're already wet."

"Really?" Penelope asked with a grin. "It's cold."

"I know. Just think of it as invigorating."

"Okay… Invigorating?"

"Come on," Marshall prompted. "Don't look at me like that. It's a beautiful morning. Birds are singing, the sun is sparkling on the bay, and we're here. Together. We might as well enjoy ourselves with a little swim."

"Why don't we go up to the pool then?" Penelope asked.

"Because we're too dirty for that. The pool guy would curse us. And Reggie wouldn't be pleased."

"Fine. The lake it is," Penelope agreed. "But you might have to haul me out again."

"That's what I'm counting on," Marshall said, his mouth turned up in a smile as he stood. "Now get ready, because I'm pushing you off this dock in 3… 2…"

"Would you do such a thing? After Hana… ?"

"Indeed, I would. This time will be fun. You'll see."

Marshall continued his countdown, then wrapped his arms around Penelope's waist as both of them went tumbling back into the water. Their heads dipped underwater, but soon breached the surface again, giggles and laughter filling the air.

As she treaded water, Penelope felt as if she was in a weird time warp. Things had changed so fast. Last night, she had been going through the motions at the party. Then there had been Audrey and a glimpse into a far more sinister world. Then her friends and their resistance. And now Marshall. She wished she could skip over everything else that would follow and stay with him.

"Tell me what happened at the police station," Penelope prompted, getting down to business. "Does the Rosemary Run force have jurisdiction here?"

"Yeah, they do. I went in and gave a statement. That's all. I didn't even speak to the detectives yet. A clerk named Pamela Woo asked me a few basic questions. I expect they'll be back in touch soon."

"Where's Reggie?"

"I'm not sure," Marshall replied. "They kept him longer. He gave a statement, too, but said he had to take care of something. I'm not sure how much police know about Reggie's operation at this point."

Penelope winced. The water was cold, but it wasn't bothering her much this time. Her mind was focused on other matters. Marshall had been right. The water was invigorating.

"Do you know what happened to Audrey?" she asked quietly.

"No. And you know I'd tell you if I did."

"Yeah, I know."

Marshall swam closer to Penelope, positioning himself just inches away. She could feel the heat from his body.

"Is that what you and the ladies were talking about before Hana pushed you in?"

Penelope nodded. "It was. I wanted the four of us to get our stories straight. I don't know what the rest of them saw. Only a little that Cheryl told us about. I saw… Things that I probably shouldn't have."

"Are you afraid, Pen?"

Penelope considered her answer before she spoke. She wasn't usually one to confide her feelings.

"A little."

Marshall wrapped one arm around Penelope and pulled her close. His strength was enough to keep her afloat. All she had to do was rest, cradled in his embrace.

"Don't be afraid," he said. "I'd never let anything happen to you."

Penelope sighed, the romance of it all washing over her and making her go weak in the knees. As she gazed into Marshall's eyes, she couldn't help herself. It felt like now or never.

She lifted her head and kissed him, more passionately this time. Their lips pressed against each other hungrily. The desire between them was electric. Penelope squared herself up in front of Marshall and wrapped her arms tightly around his neck. Her dress floated upwards around her waist, but she didn't care. She let it happen.

They kissed, long and tenderly, while Marshall slowly swam them closer to shore until finally, he reached a depth where he could stand. Once their heads and shoulders were safely above water and he had gained solid footing, he let his hands reach under Penelope's dress and grip her firm backside. He wanted her. Badly. She knew just how much as his firmness reached towards her, throbbing with life and aching to be invited in.

Penelope throbbed, too, the pressure between her legs intensifying until she thought she might burst. She wanted to feel Marshall inside of her. It seemed like she always had. She'd dreamed of this day. Aside from Audrey and Reggie and a brewing police investigation, it was every bit as magical as she'd imagined.

"Take me," she whispered between kisses, her hands meeting his and guiding them underneath her panties.

"Are you sure?" he asked. "Like this?"

She moved one palm to his manhood and stroked it firmly, paying special attention to the sensitive tip. "Exactly like this. Do it now, Marshall Erving. I want you."

Without so much as a glance over their shoulders to see if anyone was watching, Marshall reached down and tore at the zipper of his pants, freeing his cock into the open water. Penelope moved her mouth around to one of his earlobes and down his neck, nibbling in all the right places as she continued to stroke. Marshall took a finger and gently moved Penelope's panties to one side, allowing him access. He paused to finger her folds and stimulate her soft bud before grabbing her hips with both hands and ramming himself into her.

It was pure ecstasy for them both. Penelope wrapped her legs around Marshall's waist and he drove deeper and deeper inside. Birds continued to chirp and the sun continued to shine as they consummated a physical union that had been years in the making. It felt natural, as if the two of them belonged in nature, making love vigorously, the same as wild animals.

They heaved and gyrated, savoring every glorious sensation as they hurried towards blessed release. Penelope climaxed first, unable to squelch her cries of delight. She moaned and writhed in front of Marshall for what seemed like a long, delicious while, making his orgasm that much more intense. When he finally burst, it was with the intensity of a fire hose, his liquid more forceful and filling than any Penelope had known. They held each other, muscles tensed, in their own world where they remained oblivious to much of what was happening around them.

Until they heard a voice nearby. Someone had been watching.

"Penelope? Marshall?"

5

Penelope nuzzled her head into Marshall's neck and kept her tight grip on him. She was experiencing the most incredible afterglow of her life. She'd been waiting on this moment for so long. She didn't want to be interrupted. And she wasn't sure she even cared who had been watching. Marshall didn't turn either. He continued to hold Penelope, their bodies intertwined. Neither of them felt the cold anymore.

"Um, what's happening in there?"

It was a woman's voice. Penelope could tell that much. She wondered if she ignored the woman, she might go away.

"Leave us be, Hana," Marshall said, his posture steady. "This doesn't concern you."

Penelope wondered how he knew Hana's voice without looking. Earlier, she'd known Hana's hands on her back. But something was different about the woman's voice now. It sounded strained. Suspecting trouble, Penelope turned to face her.

"What?"

"I need help," Hana said.

Penelope looked at Marshall skeptically. "I'm not sure if we should believe her."

Marshall turned, eyeing Hana without loosening his hold on Penelope.

"Look," Hana began. "I don't care about the two of you in there like that. We've all known you're in love with each other. That's old news. You have been for years. And Marshall, we figured there was some other reason you married Reggie. You don't love him like you love Pen. So blah, blah, blah, and congratulations. Let's move on, shall we?"

Penelope and Marshall looked at each other. Marshall shrugged, indicating his agreement.

"Alright," Penelope said, moving away from Marshall in the water and getting her clothing turned around properly again. "What do you need help with?"

"Yeah," Marshall added. "What's wrong? Because from where I'm sitting, you probably deserve whatever trouble you're in. You've been a real prick."

Hana scowled. Even in her time of need, she was abrasive to deal with. She didn't have the good sense to be humble. She put a hand on one hip. "I saw someone. Behind the hedges on the front lawn."

"When?" Marshall asked.

"Maybe it was the gardeners," Penelope offered.

"It wouldn't be them," Marshall explained. "The yard and gardens were all prepped for the party yesterday. There's nothing left for them to do for at least a week."

Hana glanced behind her. "Could you two get out of

the water? I'm uncomfortable here alone."

Penelope chuckled. What sweet revenge this was, and she hadn't even needed to dish it up herself. It was long past time that someone or something took Hana down a peg. She was too conceited and detached for her own good.

Marshall nodded, fastening his pants then helping Penelope to the shore. They looked flush as they stepped out of the water, whether from sun exposure or physical exertion. No one could deny that the pair looked happy. That was a good thing, if unexpected on this particular day.

Hana gestured towards the dock, and Marshall and Penelope followed. Hana let the two of them have the chairs. She stood with her back to the bay while they wrung their clothes out and spread the fabric for maximum exposure to the warm breeze.

"What?" Penelope asked the woman. "Afraid to face the water in case I might push you in?"

Penelope felt emboldened with Marshall at her side. Finding the nerve to make sweet love to him hadn't hurt either.

"I'm sorry about that," Hana said in a rare admission of guilt. "I shouldn't have."

"Thank you," Penelope replied.

"Yeah, thank you," Marshall echoed. "That's better."

Hana smiled briefly, then began to fidget with a fingernail again.

"So, now you want to get serious about our situation?" Penelope asked.

"I do."

"Just to be clear," she continued. "You couldn't be bothered when it was only Audrey's ass in danger. But now you see someone on the front lawn and you're freaked out."

"You don't have to make me sound so selfish," Hana returned.

"Oh, you do that all on your own," Marshall added, raising his brows.

Hana slumped her shoulders, then sat down on the dock. Penelope thought she suddenly looked small. Like a young child instead of a grown woman. Fear will shrink even the strongest and tallest among us.

"I get it," Hana said. "But it's time to be serious. Like Pen said earlier. I did see something last night. And now… well, I'm afraid that someone might want to keep me from talking about what I know."

"Okay," Penelope replied. "I'm glad we're on the same page. But that's quite a leap, isn't it? When I mentioned someone coming after us, I didn't envision them hiding in the hedges."

Marshall shrugged like he wasn't so sure Hana was wrong. "I don't know," he said. "I've seen things around this place that would surprise you both. I can vouch for danger lurking."

"Seriously?" Penelope asked.

"Yeah, seriously," he confirmed.

"So, you're saying a bad guy— for lack of a better description— could realistically be hiding in the hedges to silence us before we tell anyone what we saw."

"Possibly. But I meant what I said, Pen. I won't let anything happen to you."

Penelope swooned. Hana rolled her eyes.

"Great. That makes me even more concerned," Hana muttered under her breath.

"How about you ladies share what you saw?" Marshall asked.

Hana answered without skipping a beat. "I'm not so sure I should. Especially now."

Marshall shook his head in frustration. "I'm not the bad guy," he said. "You came back here, interrupting, and asked for help. How are we supposed to help you if we don't know what's going on?"

"Agreed," Penelope added. "My sentiments exactly."

Hana remained silent.

"Then let's do it this way," Marshall tried, scooting to the front of his chair. "Let's go look for the guy out front. If we find him, I'll ask some questions and assess the threat."

"No!" Hana exclaimed. Her reaction surprised them.

Marshall took a breath. Penelope followed his lead, inhaling deeply, then exhaling. She had to be conscious of her breath when in stressful situations.

"Should we go to the police?" Penelope asked Marshall.

"No," he said swiftly. "We don't want to draw any more suspicion to ourselves and the things that happen on this property. You know that."

"I know," Penelope said. "But this is important. It's different."

"Different how?" Marshall returned.

"Different because a young woman disappeared… or was murdered…"

"We don't know that, Pen," Marshall answered. "I don't know that, anyway. Do you? Because I didn't see anything suspicious."

Penelope chewed her bottom lip. She thought about how she wasn't good at lying. And she didn't want to lie to Marshall. But she wasn't sure she wanted to speak freely with Hana anymore. She didn't feel safe.

"Um, well…" Penelope began. "Maybe we should talk about that privately."

Hana's eyes flicked upwards. "Hey…" she began.

"If you're more comfortable that way, then of course," Marshall reassured, reaching up and smoothing Penelope's hair. "It'll be just us."

"Guys…" Hana tried again, the color draining from her face.

"I think I am," Penelope replied, oblivious to Hana's distress. Hana was a drama queen. Like the boy who cried wolf.

"Guys!" Hana yelled now, pointing to the hill behind them.

Marshall and Penelope turned, not expecting the sight that awaited them.

There, coming down the hillside towards the dock, was Reggie, his deep brown skin glistening with perspiration as his large nostrils flared. But that wasn't what frightened them. Walking beside Reggie and carrying what looked like a weapon in his pants pocket was a huge blonde-haired man in a suit. He was at least as tall as Marshall. He towered over Reggie. Penelope couldn't tell if Reggie was with the big man voluntarily, or if the man was forcing Reggie to follow his instructions.

6

"That's him!" Hana said in a shrill whisper. "The guy from the front lawn."

"This guy was hiding in the hedges?" Marshall asked in disbelief. "Really?"

"Yes!" Hana confirmed. She slid forward, cowering behind Marshall.

Marshall stood up tall, puffing his chest out and using both arms to tuck Penelope and Hana behind him.

As the blonde man got closer, he reminded Penelope of the Russian from the Rocky Balboa movies she used to watch with her dad when she was a kid. He was menacing. She thought he couldn't possibly be with Reggie. Could he?

"Who's this?" Marshall asked his husband, his voice deep and firm. "And why is he here?"

"Not now," Reggie said as the two men approached the dock. He grimaced.

It was apparent that Reggie was there against his will. Penelope could see it all clearly as she peeked around

Marshall. The blonde man did, in fact, have a gun, and he was pointing it at Reggie.

Marshall's posture stiffened. "Talk to me, Reggie. What does this man want?"

The blonde man grunted, motioning behind Marshall. "The girl," he growled. "Give her to me and no one will get hurt."

Penelope sucked in a gulp of air. She wasn't sure which girl he was talking about. Terror struck her like a bolt of lightning and held onto her. Her mind spun at a dizzying pace as she tried to think. She'd been at the mercy of men before. She wasn't a stranger to that. She'd even dealt with angry men who were aggressive towards her. But this seemed far more frightening than anything she'd ever seen. This man was on a mission. It seemed like he'd be willing to hurt anyone who got in his way. Penelope shook with fear. Her only comfort was knowing that Marshall would keep her safe. She believed that much.

"I don't think so," Marshall said. "These ladies aren't going anywhere. Not as long as I'm here to have a say in it."

"The dark one," the blonde-haired man shouted. "Now! Or people will get hurt."

Hana yelped. "I didn't see anything! I don't know anything! I swear."

She reached out for Marshall and practically climbed him like a tree. Marshall bore her weight, allowing her refuge behind him.

"Dammit, Marshall," Reggie grunted. "Don't try to be

a hero, for Christ's sake. Do what he says. Give him the girl."

Marshall looked at Reggie, an expression of disappointment on his face. He wrinkled his nose. "Is that how it's going to be, Reggie? You're going to sacrifice your own people now?"

Reggie shook his head as the blonde man moved the gun in his direction. "I don't see what choice we have."

Hana suddenly sobbed, her usual cocky demeanor shattered. Penelope remained still and silent, hoping not to draw attention to herself. Neither of the ladies had any idea what to do. They felt physically vulnerable and unable to even put up a decent fight. At least, not compared to Marshall. He was the one who had options. They weren't good options, but they were options, nonetheless.

"We always have a choice," Marshall said.

"Spoken like a hero," Reggie mumbled. "We don't. *You* don't."

Penelope feared for Marshall's safety and her own, but she suddenly remembered something about him that she hadn't thought about in a long time.

Marshall once told her he had served four years in the U.S. Marine Corps. He hadn't wanted to make a career out of the military, so he'd enlisted for a four-year term and then gotten out when that term was finished. Marshall wasn't the type to talk about it much. He didn't wear Marine Corps t-shirts or have a bumper sticker on his truck. He was humble, never one to brag. But one warm August night a couple of years ago, when he and Penelope had been drinking beer and telling stories, he had told her about his service. Maybe his training could be put to use now.

Acting out of instinct, Penelope nudged Marshall in the small of his back from behind, poking as if she had to tell him something. He turned his head ever so slightly, acknowledging her.

"Be brave, my dear," she whispered. "I believe in you. Semper Fi."

Hana didn't react. But the words seemed to give Marshall the boost of confidence he needed. He stood up even straighter, his hands balling into fists.

"Okay," Marshall said to the blonde man. "She's right here. If you promise not to hurt anyone else, you can take her. I see now that my husband is right. We don't have any other choice. Since you have a gun. You win."

"What?" Hana screeched, clawing as she pulled herself further onto Marshall's back.

"Trust him," Penelope whispered, hoping the blonde man couldn't hear. Hana's body relaxed just enough to allow herself faith in her friends.

The blonde man grunted and moved forward. "No funny business," he instructed. His voice was gruff, as if he'd been chain smoking most of his life. There was an edge to it.

"Nothing like that," Marshall assured.

Penelope began to crack under the pressure as she sipped air, her body threatening to reveal the lie that wasn't even hers to tell.

Sip. Sip. Hold.

The blonde man continued toward the middle of the dock, one slow and deliberate step at a time.

In a burst, Penelope pushed out the air once she could no longer hold it. "Pfftt," she blurted.

The blonde man tilted his head to one side. "What's wrong with her?" he asked.

Marshall used a hand to squeeze Penelope's arm, urging her to keep it together. "Easy now. She has asthma. It flares up when she gets nervous. Nothing to worry about. You said you wanted the other girl, anyway."

Another lie. Penelope didn't have asthma.

Sip. Sip. Sip.

She knew Marshall would move soon. Only now it was a balancing act. Penelope wondered if he'd be able to formulate a plan of attack before she gave him away with her ridiculous breathing routine. She silently scolded herself.

"Give me the girl," the blonde man said again, turning his gun to Marshall. "I'm running out of patience."

"Okay, okay," Marshall said, holding his posture. "She's scared. Take it slow and easy."

There was a moment of tense silence as the man stepped closer. Reggie paused at the edge of the dock and stood with his shoulders slumped. It didn't look like he intended to put up a fight.

Sip. Sip.

"Slow and easy," Marshall repeated.

Penelope held it in. She felt herself getting lightheaded, but she held it in.

Hana remained silent, clutching Marshall.

The blonde man stepped closer, inch by inch, pointing his gun, until finally, he came within arm's reach of Marshall.

On impulse, Penelope used all of her air to shout as loud as she could. "Over there!" she exclaimed, pointing towards the house. At the same time, she grabbed Hana's arms, freeing Marshall.

The blonde man glanced in the direction Penelope was pointing. He was no amateur. He didn't turn his head all the way around. But the glance was enough to allow Marshall the advantage.

Marshall surged forward, taking hold of the end of the weapon and directing it away from the people. Shots rang out as the two men struggled for control. Hana clung to Penelope. The ladies stood, trapped on one end of the deck and unable to make their way to the grassy yard until the men moved off the path.

"Get down!" Marshall yelled.

Hana did as instructed, throwing herself down hard on the deck. But Penelope stood. Although she couldn't explain why, she knew she wanted to help. She realized it was probably a foolish move. She hadn't been trained in physical combat. Yet she wanted to do something. She didn't want to leave Marshall to this alone. A quick glance at Reggie told her he wasn't planning to assist. He remained limp and useless, most likely in shock. He would not rise to the occasion.

The blonde man grunted with effort, lowering his brow. He twisted and pulled Marshall towards him, like a wrestler wrapping up an opponent. Marshall wasn't just any opponent, though. He was strong and skilled. It took less than a minute for him to get the gun away and hurl it into the bay.

Now the true hand to hand combat began. The men

crouched in front of each other, fighters at the ready. Without words, they continued on, Marshall making the first move as he rushed the blonde man. Marshall grappled with the man, wrapping his arms around his waist and working to knock him off balance. As they spun, Penelope saw her chance and sprang into action.

She screamed like a banshee and rushed into the fray, jumping on the blonde man's back and wrapping her arms around his neck. Her dress ripped as she leapt, but that didn't matter now. She raised her hands and clawed at the man's face from behind, feeling for soft tissue. Her fingers quickly found his eyes, and she dug in as hard as she could with her long fingernails.

The blonde man screamed in pain and tried to swat Penelope away. Only Marshall was plowing forward, determined to bring him to the ground. In a tangle of arms and legs, the three of them fell hard against the dock. Penelope kept her tight hold, gripping the man's torso tightly with her legs as she scratched at his eyes. She could feel his eyeballs being destroyed. They oozed and squished. She didn't hesitate. This man had threatened their very lives. So what if she took his vision? At least, she'd live to tell the tale.

"I've got him," Marshall shouted as he went for the man's throat. "Go, Pen. Get to safety."

Satisfied that she'd done what she could, Penelope released her grip and scurried back to lay face down on the dock near Hana. Her braid was undone, and her dress tattered. She was a disheveled mess now, but she felt like a proud warrior.

"Wow," Hana mouthed as her friend plopped beside her.

The blonde man lay belly up as Marshall straddled him and used both hands to compress his throat. Penelope wasn't sure if Marshall aimed to kill him, but she wouldn't blame him if he did. The man's eyes bled. His hands alternated between instinctively covering the sockets and trying to pry Marshall's hands off his throat. It seemed like Marshall had complete control now. The man writhed in pain. He was nearly ready to give up. But not before one last surge of energy.

The blonde man arched his back and threw himself sideways, launching Marshall off of him and sending both of them into the water.

"Oh, no!" Hana exclaimed, jumping up to get a better view.

"Jesus!" Reggie said from a distance, not moving to help.

Without even thinking, Penelope rushed forward, jumping into the water to help.

In a series of splashes, the three of them emerged above the surface, Marshall and the blonde man struggling against each other. The blond man had to be blind at this point, which gave Marshall the advantage. But the man was strong, too, and he wasn't giving up without a fight. The minute Penelope got her bearings, she swam towards the man, again jumping on his back. This time was even easier since the buoyancy of the water aided her leap.

"Pen!" Hana yelled from the shore. "Be careful!"

Marshall glanced at Penelope and nodded, his expression one of pride.

Taking Marshall's nod as permission, Penelope used her lanky arms to put the blonde man in a choke hold. She'd never seen such a thing before, except on TV. She placed one elbow strategically on the front of his throat and braced that arm with the other. Then she squeezed as hard as she could. Marshall held the man's arms from the front as he thrashed. Penelope could feel the life drain out of him. She continued to squeeze, harder and harder, until his body went completely limp and he was lifeless.

Penelope locked eyes with Marshall as the two of them let the man go. He slipped quietly into the bay and beneath their reach where he couldn't hurt them anymore.

7

For more than an hour, Penelope, Hana, and Marshall sat motionless on the dock. They had been too rattled to bother with the chairs, but had instead sat right on the hot planks. It was mid-morning now, and they'd soon be burnt by the sun, if they weren't already. Physical sensations were dulled for all three of them. Things that usually mattered didn't matter. They didn't even feel the heat from the planks or the overhead sun. Not really.

Reggie had disappeared, throwing his arms up and fleeing to the safety of the house not long after the blonde man sank. The others wondered what he was doing. Although they weren't concerned enough to follow him and find out. They weren't sure whose side he was on. And they couldn't be certain he wasn't their enemy.

Reggie was the one who'd gotten them into this mess in the first place. He had to have been. This whole operation was his doing. His baby. Everyone else had been swept up. Including Marshall.

Hana was the first to speak.

"What now?" she asked. It was a simple question, but one that didn't have an easy answer.

"I wish I knew," Penelope said. She was rattled, but she was also proud of herself. She had always wondered how she'd react if her life was in danger. She'd passed her own test, and by her own metrics, she'd done it with flying colors.

"You two were good," Hana said. "I froze like a stupid little baby."

"Don't be so hard on yourself," Penelope replied. "The chips were down. It was a tough situation."

"Yeah."

Hana fiddled with a fingernail. It was her go-to move when she was nervous. Penelope was surprised she hadn't torn her fingernails completely off by now.

Marshall gingerly traced his knuckles where the skin was broken and bruised.

"Does it hurt?" Penelope asked, leaning on his shoulder.

"Not really," he replied. "How are your fingers?"

Penelope held them up like a kid showing hands to a parent. They were covered in dried blood. She wasn't sure if it was her own or the blonde man's. "I think I might have jammed a finger. I should probably get it looked at."

Marshall scooped her hands inside of his and pulled them to his lips, kissing them gently. "I don't like seeing you hurt."

"I'm okay. Nothing that won't heal."

"No kidding," Hana added. "That could have been so much worse."

Marshall nodded without taking his eyes off Penelope.

"Like I asked," Hana continued. "What now? Someone has to decide. We can't sit on this dock in the sun forever."

Penelope chuckled. "Too bad."

Marshall looked at her as if he wanted to laugh, too, but he thought better of it.

"I'm sorry," Penelope said. "I shouldn't laugh. This isn't funny. At all." She scooted closer to Marshall and wrapped one arm around him.

The ladies were waiting on Marshall to take the lead. He had proven his prowess in physical combat, and they assumed his training had taught him strategy, too. He knew they were waiting on him. And he knew he was best prepared to figure out next steps. Further, he understood the cruel way life sometimes called you to fulfill a duty whether you wanted to or not. He had answered that call when he joined the Marines. He wasn't about to walk away now. Not that he could if he'd wanted to.

"We have two choices," he began.

"Right!" Hana said, happy for the direction.

"We can call the police."

"I'm not opposed to that," Penelope said. "You guys have security cameras out here, don't you? Footage will prove that we were acting in self-defense."

"We do," Marshall confirmed. "But we can't be sure that Reggie hasn't already destroyed the tape."

Hana looked puzzled.

Penelope wasn't surprised. "You think he's in on this somehow?"

Marshall shrugged. "Not so much in on it as in the

middle of it. I think someone is pulling his strings. Maybe blackmailing him."

"Wow," Hana mused. "The shit keeps getting deeper."

"So, if he's destroyed the footage…" Penelope said.

"And if he'll contradict our version of what happened…" Marshall added. "Then we could be in a lot of trouble with the police. Reggie is well connected. I suspect he'd be able to make things go his way."

"Damn," Penelope said. She put one hand over her mouth as she thought about it all. "You know I can't lie without the breathing thing. Maybe if we tell the police about that, they'll believe me. I could demonstrate and everything."

Marshall shrugged again. "I know, Pen. I think this is more serious than convincing the police."

"You do?"

"Yes, just like you were saying earlier. If someone wants to silence us, they won't play nice. And that will be a far greater threat to our lives than the police. Hell, we might be safer in jail, for that matter."

Hana stood and paced. She couldn't seem to help it. She dragged her feet as she shuffled back and forth, chewing her fingernails.

"Hana, what is it?" Penelope asked.

Hana shook her head.

"You know you have to tell us," Penelope prompted. "We're in this too deep. We just murdered a man."

"No," Hana clarified. "You two murdered a man. I just watched."

"That still makes you an accessory," Marshall added.

"Just tell us," Penelope continued. "I know you saw

something last night related to Audrey's disappearance. I saw something, too. And I assume that's why the brute came after you. If he knows, someone else does. It's only a matter of time before they send another assassin."

"Assassin?" Hana asked.

"What else should I call him? That guy was a professional. No doubt about it."

"Fine," Hana said. "Whatever. This is so bizarre. It's like an episode of The Twilight Zone right now. None of it feels real. I want out."

"That's how it happens sometimes," Marshall said. "Life can turn on a dime. There will be time for bellyaching about it later. Right now, we have to buck up and deal with it. I agree with Penelope. You need to tell us what you know. Stop wasting time."

Hana paced back and forth a few more times. She dragged her feet so hard Penelope thought she might wear a hole in the dock. Finally, she took a deep breath and steeled herself for the inevitable discussion.

"I'm just going to say it," Hana blurted. "I saw a man put something in Audrey's drink. It was liquid, or maybe powder. Whatever it was, it dissolved right away. It was in a little flask."

"Oh, no," Penelope muttered.

"Then a little while later, I saw another man with Audrey near the pool. She seemed out of it. She was stumbling around. She could barely stand. But the man led her into the pool with him. He propped her up so no one around them realized how bad off she was."

"Oh…"

"And then I saw when he let her go under. He moved

in front of her to block the view, but I saw. I thought I was hidden behind one of the round columns on the patio, but he noticed me. We locked eyes. I froze like a deer in headlights, until right then, Cheryl showed up and asked me what I was looking at. She snapped me out of it. That's when I went outside to call 9-1-1."

"So that was you?" Marshall asked.

"I didn't know what else to do," Hana explained. "I wanted to get Audrey help. I was scared."

"I get it," Marshall said. "It's just... dicey... because, well, you know."

"I know!" Hana said emphatically. "I wouldn't have called authorities if I'd thought there was any other way. Audrey's life was in danger."

Penelope lifted her hand to tousle the front of Marshall's short hair. He kept a closely cropped haircut, much like what he'd worn as a Marine. "It's an impossible situation," she said. "We can't blame Hana for calling for help."

"I know," Marshall said. "I hate that I'm involved in this. It was attractive in the beginning. Easy money. And it didn't seem like anyone could get hurt. Now look at us."

"I felt the same way," Hana confirmed. "Reggie made it sound safe. And easy. Now we're in a web of lies and deceit that I'm afraid we won't be able to escape."

"Lies?" Penelope said. "I know what happens here is secret, but I haven't had to lie about it. I'm not sure I could..."

"We know," Marshall inserted. "We know."

"Yes, lies," Hana confirmed. "I've lied. Lots of times. We try to do the lying so you don't have to."

"Gosh. I didn't know."

Hana sat back down next to Penelope, her appearance largely unchanged since the night before. Penelope marveled at how put together Hana looked while she was a torn-apart mess.

"Alright," Marshall began again, his plan coming together. "I don't know all that Reggie is into. I promise to tell you two everything I know. I've made up my mind, though. I don't want to be part of it anymore. It isn't right. And now it's turned deadly. I want to go to the police. But first, we need to do some investigating on our own. I want to draw out every last henchman who might come after us. When the police hear our story, I want to deliver all the bad guys, even if that includes Reggie. I love him, but I can't be with him anymore. I can't go along with his schemes anymore."

"Aw," Penelope said with a sigh.

"If I get out of this thing alive," Marshall continued. "I want to sleep at night without worrying that someone is coming to kill me. And I want that for the two of you. Are you with me?"

"Absolutely," Penelope replied. "I agree completely."

She thought about the little blue house with a big yard and the puppies. She didn't want assassins spoiling her dream life once it came to fruition. She'd help Marshall to root them out now. Then they could leave the shadows once and for all. Reggie's high-end escort service would either go on without them or it wouldn't. But Penelope was done. Just like Marshall. She wouldn't allow her time and attention to be sold. And she wouldn't recruit girls. Not anymore. She'd find honest work that didn't exploit anyone. Even if that meant upsetting Cheryl, who had gotten her involved with Reggie's service in the first place. Even if it meant that she went back to being broke. And even if it meant living within meager means, like her childhood. She'd figure something out. She'd find a better way.

8

The next morning, Penelope opened her eyes to see Marshall sleeping next to her. The finger injury she'd sustained struggling with the blonde man was barely noticeable now. She smiled as she remembered the events of the day before and how Marshall had come back to her condo in Rosemary Run to spend the night. He had told Reggie he was leaving, and he needed a place to stay. It only made sense that the two of them would stay together. In fact, it only made sense that the two of them would *be* together, an official couple. Like Hana had said, they'd been in love for years. Everyone had known it.

Marshall rolled over and stretched, smiling just as big as Penelope. His broad, long body filled up her queen bed.

"Good morning, beautiful," he said as he pulled her in for a kiss.

The sheet slid down as they moved, exposing Penelope's bare breasts. She had been naked in front of plenty of men before. She knew her body was enticing to them, even if she wasn't a world-class beauty like her friends. She felt confident and sexy in front of Marshall now. The electricity between them felt both familiar and brand new. They'd never been together like this before.

"Good morning to you," she echoed. "I can hardly believe this is real. You're here."

"Nowhere else I'd rather be."

Marshall had taken off his wedding ring. There was a tan line that remained. It bothered Penelope a little. Mostly, she understood, though. She and Marshall had been friends long before he had met Reggie. She'd been there to see how it had happened.

"I know," Marshall said when he saw Penelope eyeing his ring finger. "I'm sorry, Pen. It should have been you and me all along."

She scooted closer to him, running one finger along his bottom lip.

"Shh," she said. "It's okay. I'm just happy that circumstances brought us together like this. I guess being in real danger has a way of making one focus on what's most important in life."

"I'd say so. But let the record note that I tried to woo you before. Oh, how I tried. You're my girl, Pen. My best girl. My one and only. I only gave up when I thought there wasn't a chance. And now, you've made me the happiest man in the world."

They nuzzled together, their bodies pressed against each other and their legs intertwined underneath the covers. They had made love the night before, then had fallen asleep, tired but satisfied. Marshall's morning erection said he was ready for more.

"Someone's energetic this morning," Penelope laughed as she kissed him again, deeply this time.

"Are you talking about this?" Marshall teased as he moved closer, pressing his rock-hard shaft between her legs.

"I am," Penelope said, wiggling with anticipation. "I think I might like to be the lucky lady who gets to feel your morning energy inside of me. If you want to share it."

"Oh, I certainly do," Marshall replied. Then he lifted the covers and crawled down Penelope's body, letting his mouth rest on top of her slippery opening. He paused, toying with her and increasing her level of desire.

"Don't stop," she said, guiding his head.

"Are you telling me you like this?" he asked as he slipped his tongue inside, swirling it around her throbbing bud.

Penelope moaned and arched her back. She'd had good sex before. Although she doubted any would now compare to sex with Marshall. After just two lovemaking sessions, he had already ruined her for all others. He was attentive in a way that no man had been. He made her feel like they weren't two individuals, but rather one interconnected being. He made her feel truly and thoroughly loved.

"I love it so much," she replied.

"Good, then I'll keep going," he whispered.

Marshall licked and sucked as Penelope became wetter and wetter. He delighted in her juices and made himself comfortable there, bringing her to mind-blowing orgasm more than once. When she was ready for him to enter her, she guided him up and took his rod in her hand. She shimmied down in the bed to position herself, then licked the length of the shaft a few times, her hand stimulating the bottom while her tongue focused on the tip. Marshall was so hard Penelope thought he might burst right then and there in her mouth.

"Get in me," she said as she hoisted herself back up to meet his lips. "I want you in me. *Now*."

"No place I'd rather be," he said again.

Marshall entered Penelope, her insides quivering with pleasure at his touch. She lifted her legs high and wrapped them around his waist as he drove into her hard and fast. He didn't close his eyes, preferring instead to take her beauty in. Seeing Penelope's naked body and feeling her soft, smooth skin was incredibly arousing to Marshall. It had been a while since he'd been with a woman. He'd always considered himself bisexual, but had recently suspected he preferred a woman's touch. He knew he'd have time to sort that out later. He wasn't sure it mattered, really, as long as Penelope knew how much he desired and loved her.

"I love the hell out of you," he mumbled as he continued to grind.

Again, Penelope swooned, this being what she had dreamed about for so long. "Marshall Erving, I love you, too."

Full to the brim with feel-good endorphins, they heaved, shook, and rubbed together until they climaxed, Marshall first and then Penelope in ecstasy as his liquid filled her.

When they were finished, Marshall rolled over. They

lay beside each other, and stared up at the ceiling, exhilarated.

"You told me you loved me," Penelope said with a giggle. "Did you mean it?"

"I do love you. Of course, I meant it. I've loved you for a long time now, Pen. I could probably remember the exact day I realized my feelings for you, if I tried."

"That's sweet," Penelope said. "I could probably do the same."

"Wait," Marshall said, leaning on one elbow. "You knew you loved me... before? And you said nothing?"

"Guilty."

"Pen! I could have skipped the entire Reggie chapter. Which means you could have, too. I'm the one who got you roped into the escort thing. Wouldn't it have been better to skip that?"

"I guess," she replied. "It's hard to say that time spent wasn't worthwhile. There's always learning to be done. We wouldn't be who we are today if we hadn't been involved with Reg and the escort service. I don't think it's helpful to look back with regret."

"But... what about Audrey... and the man at the bottom of the bay?"

"I don't know. We'll sort it all out. Together. We're in this together."

Just then, Penelope's phone rang. She recognized the name and photo saved in the caller ID from across the room. It was Cheryl. Cheryl never called unless it was important, preferring to text or message through social media instead.

"I have to get that," Penelope said as she stood and

walked to pick up her phone. She didn't bother covering herself, prompting Marshall to whistle and wink as she walked. "Hush," she said, smiling. "Seriously, though, it's Cheryl. And she only calls when it's important."

"Huh," Marshall said. "Seemed important that she should stand up for you yesterday when Hana was giving you a hard time."

"You're right," Penelope said. "Let me see what she has to say."

She lifted a finger in the air to tell him to stay quiet, then she pushed the button to connect the call.

9

"Cheryl? What's up?"

"Pen! I'm glad you answered. I need to talk to you. Right away. Can I come over?"

Penelope looked around her condo at the clothes strewn all over the place. She lived on the fifth floor of a renovated building downtown. It was too high for anyone to see through her windows from the outside which afforded her the luxury of being messy if she wanted to. Plus her view was great, especially at night. She'd have to clean up if Cheryl was coming over.

"Okay," Penelope agreed. "Give me a few minutes."

They hung up the phone, Cheryl promising to arrive in no sooner than twenty minutes.

"Does that mean I need to make myself scarce?" Marshall said. "I don't want to be in the way."

Marshall needed to get some things from Reggie's house, anyway. He knew he could use the time.

"Either way is okay with me," Penelope said. "I want you to be comfortable here. Think of this as your home now. Even though we haven't talked about those details yet, please know that you have a place with me."

Marshall grabbed Penelope and pulled her back into the bed as she neared it. "I like the sound of that."

Penelope kissed him long and slow, letting her exposed nipples brush gently against Marshall's muscular chest while her long, loose hair cascaded around his shoulders. If they'd had more time, they would have made love again. They couldn't get enough of each other.

"I think I'll go pick up a few things from Reggie's," Marshall said. "I won't be gone long. I could use the time to do a little packing. Assuming that's okay with you?"

"No worries," Penelope replied.

They quickly got showered and clothed, Penelope in a casual, heather gray cotton dress and Marshall in khaki shorts and a California state flag t-shirt. Then Marshall made the bed and scooted out the door.

Penelope was tidying up when Cheryl arrived. Cheryl clamored her way through the unlocked front door, bumping and banging as she went. If anyone else had been around, her entrance would have been quite a scene.

"Oh my God," Cheryl said as she kicked the door shut behind her with one foot. "You won't believe what has happened."

Penelope raised one eyebrow. "Try me."

She hadn't told Cheryl about the blonde man at the bottom of the bay. Or about what Hana had seen at the party. Or even about Marshall leaving Reggie.

Cheryl dove onto the couch and tossed her handbag on the coffee table. Penelope's condo had a separate bedroom and living room area. There was a tiny kitchen and a powder room by the entrance, plus a large full ensuite bathroom. Cheryl had been over hundreds of times. She felt comfortable making herself at home.

"Wait," Cheryl said, lifting her head up, sniffing the air dramatically. "It smells like a man in here... Oh, holy shit, Pen. It smells like sex in here!"

Penelope blushed. She couldn't hide her smile, but she was mortified. She didn't like talking about her sex life. Especially not to her more confident friends.

"Who is it? Did you meet someone at the party?"

"Not exactly," Penelope replied. It was the truth.

"Then who?" Cheryl continued. "Was it a client? I didn't think you had sex with clients? Aren't you booked in the look-but-don't-touch category?"

"I don't have sex with clients. And anyway, I'm not doing that anymore. I'm done."

Cheryl looked surprised. Really surprised.

"Don't look so shocked," Penelope said. "I've had enough. That's all. After what happened with Audrey... and..."

"And what?"

Penelope hesitated. She wasn't sure she should tell Cheryl everything that had happened after she'd left the dock. It wasn't that she didn't trust Cheryl, because she did. But she thought maybe it was best to keep the circle tight. The fewer people who knew, the better.

"That's it. After what happened with Audrey and how she's missing or dead, or whatever. It's got me rattled."

It felt bad to leave Cheryl out of the loop. Penelope began to sip air in anticipation of having to tell an outright lie. She wished her body wouldn't betray her like this. Besides, Cheryl knew her breathing routine and would immediately know if Penelope was lying. Her only hope was to change the subject.

"It was Marshall," Penelope blurted, before Cheryl had a chance to ask questions about Audrey and the party. "Sex. It was with Marshall. He just left a few minutes ago. I'm surprised you didn't see him on the elevator."

Cheryl sat up and scooted to the front edge of the sofa, her eyes wide. "Marshall Erving?"

"That's the one."

"You and Marshall Erving had sex in this condo? Today?"

"Yes."

"But…"

Penelope could see the wheels turning in her friend's head as she sat down on the sofa beside her. "I know. It happened fast. But I've loved him for ages. You know that."

"Does Reggie know? Poor Reggie."

"I wouldn't call Reggie poor, in any sense of that word," Penelope said. "I don't have anything against him, exactly. Nothing I can't overlook. I guess… But that's beside the point. Reggie is fine. Marshall told him yesterday. I don't think their marriage was ever more than a bad idea borne out of convenience."

"How so?" Cheryl asked.

She was dressed casually in tight-fitting jeans and a short-sleeved Bruce Springsteen t-shirt with a v-neck. Penelope thought how impossible it was that Cheryl could still look so beautiful, even in basic clothing. Cheryl was a classic beauty. Her attractiveness would fit in during any age.

"I mean that Reggie is good at convincing people to do what he wants. Just look at the escort service and how many of us he roped into participating. He wouldn't have been able to do it alone," Penelope explained. "I think Marshall got caught up in all of that. In fact, I think he let himself get caught up in it to distract from his sadness over me."

Cheryl smirked. "You think?"

Penelope shrugged. "I don't know what was wrong with me. I wanted to be with Marshall. Deep down, some part of me felt like I didn't deserve it. My mom made sure to pass her low self-esteem on to me. I've tried all of my life to shake her issues off, but I guess some of them stuck."

Cheryl put an arm around her friend. She'd been there when, as kids, Jean's anger had been directed towards Penelope. She'd seen how unfair it was.

Once, the girls had been playing a game of foursquare with a bouncy ball in Penelope's backyard when Jean came out on a tear. Zach, an infant at the time, had been napping in his stroller, parked nearby and safely shaded by a leafy tree. Penelope and Cheryl had been third graders, one nine-years-old and the other just turned ten. They had been good girls, never in trouble at school and always helpful to their teachers and friends. Cheryl had known that Penelope had a hard time at home, but she hadn't realized just how hard or else she wouldn't have come over to play.

The girls had been bouncing their ball and giggling

like kids do, Penelope keeping a dutiful eye on her baby brother. Felix had been traveling for work and wasn't due home for several more days. Jean had been sleeping inside, even though it was mid-afternoon. She had often slept most of the day and night, finding waking life unappealing. Or so Penelope had thought. She never quite understood the subtleties.

Everything had been fine, until the ball accidentally hit one of the windows in Jean's bedroom, making a loud thud and waking her up. Less than a minute later, Jean had burst out the back door in a rage, arms flailing and teeth gnashing. She had called Penelope a slew of names, including brat, pissant, and puke. Puke had been the worst. Grabbing Penelope by the elbow, Jean had dragged her into the house where she continued to berate her, unleashing a tidal wave of anger that the young girl hadn't deserved. Cheryl had been left to comfort baby Zach as Jean's voice boomed throughout the vicinity, scaring the infant.

Cheryl was one of few people who understood the extent of what Penelope had been forced to endure. None of it had been reasonable or fair. Jean hadn't beaten her daughter, but the damage to her psyche had been nearly the same. Penelope hadn't been allowed to be a kid. She'd had to grow up walking on eggshells and trying to anticipate her mother's moods in an effort to keep herself and her baby brother out of the crosshairs. The fact the Jean had loved her children and was sometimes kind was of little consequence given the way she regularly terrorized them. Cheryl knew what Penelope didn't at the time: no child deserved to be treated that way. It had been abuse. Plain and simple.

As young adults, Cheryl had been by Penelope's side, too, when Jean was killed in a car accident. Jean had been driving on a curvy road one morning as rain had begun to fall. Police had later confirmed that she had been following posted speed limits and driving safely for weather conditions. But somehow, Jean's car had hydroplaned and sent her into a spiral across the road. In a case of bad timing, a dump truck had been approaching from the other direction and was unable to swerve in time. The truck had t-boned Jean's vehicle, snapping her neck and ending her life in an instant.

Penelope had been twenty-two at the time and was unprepared for life without her mother. Cheryl had always admired Penelope's ability to focus on the positive and find ways to connect with Jean, and Penelope hadn't been ready for that to end. She'd hoped that, someday, Jean could get proper treatment for her mental health issues and that the two of them could repair their damaged relationship. On that fateful morning as rain had gently fallen, those hopes had been dashed.

It had been less than a year later when Felix had died suddenly, too. He'd had an aneurysm burst and was gone within hours. That loss had been harder for Penelope in some ways, because she and her dad had always been close. But it had been easier in others, because, at least, she knew her dad loved her. There had been nothing left unsaid.

"Aw, you're a good girl, Pen," Cheryl said. "You always have been."

"Thanks, you," Penelope replied.

Having a friend like Cheryl was a gift. She understood things that no one else did about Penelope's life, except for maybe Zach.

"You don't have to explain it to me, you know? I was there. I remember."

"I'm glad," Penelope said. "I don't know what I'd do without you in my life, Cheryl. You're my oldest friend. And my best friend."

The ladies hugged, Penelope leaning her head on Cheryl's shoulder.

"Listen," Cheryl said. "You deserve all the happiness this world will allow you. I'm happy for you and Marshall. And I'm behind you one hundred percent. Team Penshall! Whoo!"

Cheryl shook one fist in the air in celebration as Penelope laughed.

"Penshall?" Penelope asked.

"What? Do you prefer Marelope?"

They both laughed now. Couple names were ridiculous, but they were fun.

"Doesn't the man's name go first?" Penelope asked. "I'm thinking of Bennifer. Oddly enough, that's the only couple name that comes to mind at the moment."

"Hell if I know," Cheryl said, removing her arm from her friend's shoulders and slapping one knee. "It doesn't matter. The point I'm trying to make is that I support you. Life is messy. I know all too well how we can get wrapped up in things against our better judgment. Loyalties end up divided. And all sorts of drama happens. Hold on to the good."

"Thanks, friend," Penelope replied. "It means the world to me."

They smiled at each other, basking in the good vibes. Penelope wanted to hold on to every bit of good, just as Cheryl had suggested. Her life was happy right now in many ways, but that didn't mean everything was okay. She had woken up several times during the night thinking about the blonde man in the bay. She was worried about Audrey, too, and about Hana having seen too much. She suspected there was more to come. The danger might get worse before it got better.

"So," Penelope said, making direct eye contact with Cheryl and ready to get down to business. "You said you had something you wanted to talk to me about. It sounded urgent. What is it?"

Cheryl took in a deep breath, then let it out slowly.

"You know what?" she asked, chewing on her lip. "It was nothing. Nothing at all. I'm sure you have things to do. I'll get out of here so you can start your day."

10

By the time Marshall returned with a load of his belongings, it was mid-afternoon and the sun was high in the sky. Penelope had opened the windows in her condo to let the spring air in. She'd spent much of the day so far reorganizing to make room for Marshall's things.

"There she is," Marshall said as he entered, beaming.

"Hello, dear," Penelope replied.

It felt like she was on Cloud 9 where Marshall was concerned. Their interaction felt more natural than anything she'd ever experienced. At least, anything she'd experienced in a romantic relationship. The ease they enjoyed reminded her of her relationship with her dad, though not in a creepy way. She didn't have to walk on eggshells around either of the two best men in her life. She knew where they stood, and she could count on them to be there for her, no matter what. It was a beautiful thing.

Marshall set the box of clothes he was carrying down on the dining table, then rushed over to where Penelope was standing in the kitchen to kiss her passionately on the lips. He placed both hands low on her hips as he did, causing the pressure to build between her legs again. They wanted each other something fierce.

"Did you see Reggie?" Penelope asked between kisses in an effort to focus on something besides sex.

"I did," he replied. "But right now, I'm kissing you."

He moved his mouth down to her neck and gently kissed the space where her shoulder joined.

"You're too good, Marshall Erving," she breathed. He was quickly making her forget about everyone and everything else.

"Oh?" he teased. "How can I be *too* good? Is there even such a thing?"

He lowered his hands, lifting the hem of her skirt and walking his fingers up her legs underneath.

Penelope blushed. Marshall's sexy talk made her think about Cheryl having said the place smelled like sex. It would smell like sex forevermore at the rate they were going. That might not be such a bad thing.

"You're right," she said, leaning back against the kitchen counter. "There's no such thing."

Feeling playful and deciding to give in to her desires, she pulled back from Marshall's lips long enough to hop up on the counter. She wasn't wearing shoes, which made it easy to slide her panties off and down her long legs, kicking them onto the floor.

"Now you're talking," Marshall said, lifting her dress higher, then sliding his t-shirt off over his head. "I want you, Penelope Cline. I want you right now."

"Then have me," she giggled. "I'm all yours."

Marshall ducked his head and buried it between her legs, reveling in her wetness. He couldn't get enough. He licked and chewed, making mental notes of which motions elicited the strongest response from Penelope's body. He surfaced for just a moment to say, "I like you in dresses. Easy access."

Penelope laughed, then pushed his head back down where she liked it. She moaned with pleasure.

Suddenly, they heard the front door open. It was directly across from the kitchen with a plain view.

Penelope jumped, pulling her dress down as she took cover. Marshall didn't move. He held his head still, but kept his tongue going.

"Marshall, the door!"

"Um hmm," he hummed. He didn't seem to care.

"Oh, my God! Not again," a female voice said. It was Hana.

She covered her eyes, but didn't leave.

Marshall pulled back, wiping his mouth and rolling his eyes. "Hello, Hana," he said irritably. "Ever try knocking?"

"It was open," Hana said. "Besides, I have a key."

Penelope ran into the bedroom to straighten herself up, the embarrassment nearly too much for her.

"Pen," Hana said as Penelope ran past. "I'm sorry!"

Marshall shook his head.

Hana closed the door behind her, then took the same seat on the sofa that Cheryl had occupied. She sat silently for a moment while she waited on Penelope to return. Marshall took a seat in an armchair nearby. He wasn't sure whether he should be involved in whatever conversation was going to take place, but he had news to share about Reggie and figured he might as well take part.

Finally, Penelope emerged, her cheeks still flush.

"Pen…" Hana began.

"Let's not discuss it," Penelope said, holding up one palm. "Please knock from now on."

"Done," Hana agreed.

Penelope took a seat beside Hana on the sofa. She considered sitting on Marshall's lap, but thought better of it. The three of them had important matters to discuss. She would have to wait to be satisfied by Marshall. Hana's entrance had killed the mood, anyway.

"What's going on?" Penelope asked.

"I need to talk to you," Hana said. "About… yesterday… and the party…"

"Okay."

"Good," Marshall added. "Even though the— ahem — timing could have been better, I need to talk to the two of you as well."

"Who will go first?" Penelope asked.

"I will," Hana said. "I haven't talked to anybody else about what happened, but a strange woman has been following me."

"A woman?" Marshall asked. "Are you sure?"

"Positive," Hana replied. "I noticed her hanging out on the sidewalk in front of my building last night. Zeke Finley, the doorman, brought it to my attention, because she asked him about me by name."

Hana lived in a condo like Penelope. Only hers was far swankier.

"Interesting," Penelope said. "What then?"

"She was out there again this morning, just standing around like she was waiting for me to leave," Hana explained.

"What did she look like?" Marshall asked.

"That's the odd part. She had white-blonde hair, much like our guy from yesterday. She was tall, and while beautiful in an intense sort of way, she looked tough for a woman. She could have been our guy's sister, they favor each other so much."

"Huh," Marshall mused.

"That sounds like a setup for a spy movie," Penelope said. "James Bond or something, no?"

"Hey, I'm feeling the *Twilight Zone* vibes here, too, but I'm just telling you what I saw."

The three of them looked at each other intently. It was proving somewhat difficult to adjust to their new reality.

"Okay," Marshall said, propping one ankle on the opposite knee. "Did she follow you when you left the building?"

"She did," Hana said. "I told Zeke what I was doing and went out a back door, hoping she wouldn't spot me. He tried to distract her, but when I pulled my Beamer around front, she saw me. I kid you not. The woman got on a motorcycle and trailed me around town. I made a few stops to see if she'd stay close. She did."

"Did she follow you here?" Penelope asked, straightening her back to glance out an open window.

"I think so," Hana replied.

Marshall jumped up and locked the deadbolt on the front door, then closed the windows.

"Why would you lead her here?" he asked once he felt certain the place was closed up securely.

Hana rubbed her temple. "Because we agreed not to go to police yet. Where else should I have gone? It's not like she attacked or even confronted me. She's keeping her distance."

Penelope looked at Marshall. "She has a point. If not the police, who else will protect her? It has to be us. We have to stick together."

Marshall shook his head again. This was getting complicated.

"Hana," Penelope continued. "What do you make of it?"

"I wish I knew. I think someone knows what I saw at the party with Audrey. They probably want to make sure I don't talk."

"If that's true, then we're in trouble," Marshall said.

"Yeah, and we talked about this yesterday," Hana added. "Sounds like you two have been too wrapped up in your whirlwind romance to focus on what's most important right now."

"We were just…" Penelope began.

"No, she's right," Marshall said. "I should have been working on this. I let myself get distracted."

"Oh, but in a good way, dear," Penelope added. "Don't be hard on yourself. I could have done better, too."

"How do you mean?" Marshall asked. "You did great yesterday at the bay. I was proud of you."

Penelope took a deep breath, but didn't let it out. Her body was prepared to hold it if what she said next wasn't the truth.

"Pen?" Hana echoed.

"It's that… well…" she stammered.

Sip. Sip.

Penelope knew she needed to get what she'd seen out in the open with Marshall and Hana. She could trust them. She thought so, anyway.

"It's okay," Marshall assured, leaning forward and squeezing Penelope's knee.

"Yeah, I know. I'm just scared."

"We all are right now," Hana added. "Go on."

Sip.

Penelope was tempted to lie. What she'd seen was worse than what Hana had. She wished she'd never been at that party in the first place. She wished she'd been sick, or injured, or anything, really, that could have kept her home that night. She didn't want to speak the words, let alone have other people hear them.

Before she could open her mouth to describe what she'd seen, a loud knock sounded at the door.

11

Penelope's heart jumped inside her chest when she heard the sound. Her hands shook, and she perspired.

"The blonde woman?" Penelope asked.

"Maybe," Marshall said, walking to the box of his belongings at the table and retrieving a handgun. "We'll find out."

"You have a gun?" Penelope asked.

"Yeah, but don't worry. I'm trained to use it. One of the benefits of being a Marine. Truly, Pen, don't stress about it. We might need a gun, and I have one. No big deal."

Penelope looked at Hana, who raised her brows with surprise. She appeared to be in a near permanent state of shock lately. She didn't offer an opinion on the knock or the gun.

Three more knocks rang out, even louder this time. Penelope thought they might break the door down; they were pounding so hard. Whoever it was meant business.

Marshall slid behind the door, his gun raised. Using his head, he motioned for Penelope to open it. Slowly, she looked through the peephole to do as he instructed. She could see two big men, one African-American and one Caucasian. Both tall and muscular. They didn't seem like bad guys, although Penelope wasn't sure what a bad guy looked like, anyway.

"I think it's okay," she whispered, turning around and giving thumbs up to Hana.

Penelope took a deep breath, then opened the door. The men smiled and held out badges. They were cops.

Thank God, Penelope thought.

"Ms. Penelope Cline?" the dark-skinned man asked. He seemed gentle, like a dad, even.

"That's right."

"I'm Detective Luke Hemming from the Rosemary Run Police Department. This is my partner, Detective Neil Fredericks. Can we come in?"

Penelope glanced at Marshall, asking his permission. She knew they'd decided not to talk to police yet. But here they were, on her doorstep. Marshall nodded, then put his gun in the waistband of his shorts and stepped into the doorway beside her.

"Yes, you may," Penelope said, allowing them entry. "This is my… boyfriend… Marshall Erving. And on the sofa is my friend, Hana Kim."

"Pleased to meet you," Luke said as they shuffled inside. "Is there somewhere we can talk privately?"

Penelope hadn't told them where to sit, so they stood awkwardly just this side of the door. She closed and locked it behind them.

"Here, join us in the living room," Marshall said, gesturing.

Even though Luke and Neil were big men, Marshall was taller than them both. He was used to being physically dominant. Other men knew it. These two were scoping him out, though. Maybe they recognized his short haircut and demeanor as former military.

"Thank you," Luke said. He was apparently the designated good cop today. He seemed friendly and accommodating, while Neil remained expressionless.

"Ms. Cline," Luke began.

"Please… call me Penelope."

"Okay," he continued, "Penelope, we have sensitive information to discuss. Might you like to do that alone?"

"Without your boyfriend and friend present?" Neil added.

Penelope looked at Marshall, who shrugged. He knew the police might try to split them up. It was a standard tactic. They'd question them individually, then compare notes to find any discrepancies in their stories. The three of them didn't have a chance of evading police if it went down that way. The detectives were too good. Marshall also knew that it was early enough in the investigation that they wouldn't be forced to split up, yet. He shook his head no.

Penelope followed Marshall's lead. "I'm comfortable discussing whatever you want in front of my boyfriend and friend," she said.

"Alright. Good," Neil replied, walking to the living room and taking a seat in the armchair Marshall had occupied. Luke sat in a second armchair, while Penelope and Marshall sat beside Hana on the sofa.

"What can we do for you today, detectives?" Marshall asked.

Marshall acted strong and confident. Penelope liked it. She felt safe with him. She was strong in her own right, and she was brave. But she'd always wished that she didn't have to be. Not all the time, anyway. No doubt, it went back to her childhood. She'd had to grow up fast. She appreciated the chance Marshall provided her to take a supporting role. It was a relief.

Luke didn't skip a beat. "We're here investigating the disappearance of a young lady named Audrey Ward. Did you know her?"

Penelope sipped air.

Sip. Sip. Hold.

This wasn't good. The detectives had just begun, and Penelope's body threatened to betray her. She could only hope they wouldn't notice. She told herself to stay cool. She purposely avoided making eye contact with Hana or Marshall.

"I didn't know her, exactly," Penelope began. Technically true. "I heard that she was missing though. You know how fast word of something like that gets around."

"I do," Luke replied, pulling a small notepad out of the breast pocket of his jacket. Both men were wearing coats and ties.

"We all heard about it," Marshall added. "A tragedy. I hope she's found safe."

Luke eyed Marshall skeptically. He seemed to be deciding whether he liked him or not.

"Did you attend a party two nights ago at a house in Sweet Balm Bay hosted by a Mr. Reginald Johns?"

"Yes," Penelope said.

She knew there was no way to avoid that question. The police had probably already seen surveillance footage from Reggie's. Or maybe they'd gotten hold of a guest list. Either way, it would be foolish to try to pretend she wasn't there.

"All three of us were there," Marshall added, his voice protective.

Hana nodded.

"And did any of you see Ms. Ward there that night?"

Sip. Sip. Sip. Sip. Hold.

Hana jumped in to take some pressure off of her friend.

"Not that I remember," she lied.

That's what they had agreed on, after all. Although, they had agreed not to tell the police what they knew until they did some investigating of their own. They hadn't wanted to lie. Now it seemed inevitable that they do so.

"Not that you remember?" Luke asked. "Or no?"

"Not that I remember. No."

Luke furrowed his brow, then scribbled something down in his notepad as Neil looked on.

"How about you, Mr. Erving? Did you see Ms. Ward at the party?"

"No," Marshall said decisively, "and you can call me Marshall. You probably already know, but Reggie Johns was… is… my husband. I've just left him and Penelope and I are together now. But on the night of the party, I acted as co-host with Reggie. I was busy with hosting duties the whole night. It didn't leave much time to mingle with guests."

Penelope exhaled. Her breath was loud, but she hadn't started sputtering yet. She had worried about Marshall's answer, but she realized that she didn't actually know if it was a lie. They hadn't talked about what he'd seen that night. Maybe he was telling the truth. He sounded convincing.

Luke scribbled some more, then turned his attention back to Penelope.

Sip. Sip.

The stress mounted.

"Penelope, did you see Ms. Ward?"

Perspiration dotted Penelope's temples as she squirmed. Her hands sweat, too. Her stomach churned.

Sip. Hold.

Luke and Neil looked at each other, probably wondering about her breathing. Surely, they noticed it now.

"Penelope," Luke tried, "are you okay?"

Against her will, it happened. Penelope exhaled in a loud burst, buzzing her lips and sputtering. Marshall bit his lip, resisting the urge to save her. Hana, too, looked pained.

"I…" Penelope began, searching desperately for a truth or a half truth that would answer Luke's question without letting him know what she'd seen.

"Maybe a glass of water would help?" Neil asked, leaning forward in his chair.

"Good idea," Hana replied, hoping to lower the tension. "I'll get it!" She stood and quickly made her way to the kitchen.

No one spoke while she was gone. Penelope sipped the air.

Sip. Sip. Sip. Sip.

When Hana returned, she handed Penelope a large glass of water. Hana returned to her seat on the sofa, almost tripping over Neil as she did. She was nervous too.

"Penelope, do you have asthma?" Luke asked. He'd noticed. "It seems like you're having some trouble breathing."

Penelope squirmed. She felt like a wild animal, trapped and without options. She knew that she hadn't done anything wrong, but it felt like she was in trouble, anyway. If she was honest with herself, it felt like it did when Jean had been angry and had directed it at her. She knew the feeling all too well. She wished more than anything that she could someday escape it.

"No, sir," she replied. "I don't think so. I'm okay."

Luke scribbled, lowering his brow even further. He glanced at Neil, who then nodded. It was an affirmation of something only the two of them understood. Penelope didn't like it.

"Look," Luke continued, "we know that you three were at the party, and we know that you probably saw Audrey there. I understand your hesitance to get involved in this, but you have a duty to report what you witnessed."

Sip. Sip.

Penelope, Marshall, and Hana remained silent. After a few moments, Neil tried.

"We don't think you had anything to do with her disappearance, if that's what you're worried about," Neil explained. "We need to know what you saw so we can catch the person or persons who did."

"So we can keep them from harming anyone else," Luke added. "None of us want that."

Sip. Sip. Sip. Hold.

Luke turned his attention again to Hana, sensing that she knew more than she was letting on. Neil nodded, staring intently.

"Ms. Kim," Luke began.

"You can call me Hana," she chirped.

"Good, now we're all on a first name basis. You can call me Luke, and you can call my partner Neil. This is a friendly inquiry. Nothing more."

"Okay," Hana said reluctantly.

"Hana," Luke continued, leaning forward and resting his elbows on his knees. "Did you see Audrey Ward at the party hosted by Reginald Johns and Marshall Erving two nights ago?"

"You already asked me that."

"I'm asking again. Did you see Audrey Ward at the party?"

Hana broke eye contact with the detective and looked out the window. Penelope and Marshall knew what she was thinking. She was debating whether the pressure from the police investigators who obviously already knew a lot was worth telling what she knew and risking trouble with the blonde woman and any other creeps like the blonde man. It was an impossible question. Which course of action would keep them safe and protect their friends and loved ones? That's what it had come down to now. There was real danger. And none of that took into consideration the blonde man in the bay. His body could surface, literally any time. They could go to prison for murder if they didn't play this right.

"Hana?" Luke asked, his gaze piercing. "I asked you a simple question."

Hana ignored him, lifting a hand to her mouth and chewing on a fingernail. All of her nails had been bitten down to the nubs over the past couple of days.

"Hana?" Neil tried. "Are you feeling alright? You seem like something's bothering you."

Marshall cleared his throat. His urge to protect the ladies was overwhelming. The situation reminded him of Prisoner of War training he'd received in the Marines. Interrogators wishing to gain intel always went for the weaker people. It was a basic tenet of human psychology. Putting pressure on the weak members of a group was a sure way to get the stronger ones to crack, because the stronger ones usually couldn't bear to see the weak and vulnerable tortured.

"Detectives," he began, as respectfully as he could. "These ladies are scared. I'm sure you can see that. Maybe that's enough for today?"

Luke and Neil looked at Marshall knowingly. They all understood what was happening. They spoke volumes to each other with their eyes. After a few more minutes of silence, Luke spoke.

"Thank you, folks, for your time. If you think of anything else— anything at all— please get in touch."

He handed each of them a business card with his contact information, then excused himself and his partner. Marshall thanked the men and locked the deadbolt behind them. Penelope and Hana collapsed onto the sofa, exhaling deeply with relief.

It was evening before Marshall came up with a solid plan. He had parked himself at the dining room table and refused to move until next steps were traced out. He hadn't yet told the ladies what he had learned at Reggie's. One step at a time. He first needed to get them to safety.

"Okay," he said, leaning back in his chair and lacing his fingers behind his head. "I've got it. At least, I've got part of it. A lot will depend on how things go from here."

"A plan?" Penelope asked, rushing to Marshall's side. She sat in a chair next to him and leaned close.

"Yes."

Hana sat across from the couple, listening eagerly.

"Tell us," Penelope said.

Marshall nodded. "So, first things first. We have to hide. We can't have the police sniffing around until we're ready to talk. And we can't have Hana's blonde woman or anyone else tracking us. We need a base of operations where we can work undetected."

"And where will we find that?" Hana asked.

"Good question," Marshall replied. "I have a place in Oregon we can go if necessary, but I'd like to stay local if at all possible. It would be much harder to do our own investigating from out of state."

"Right," Penelope agreed.

Marshall continued. "I know a fellow jarhead who lives on the outskirts of Rosemary Run, down towards Sweet Balm Bay. We served together in Iraq. His name is Brian Patterson. I'm not completely sure of his setup, but I know he has a basement. I think he's built an attached underground bunker by now. Last I talked to him, he was making arrangements for a full scale doomsday bunker. That was a couple of years ago."

"You want us to go to a doomsday bunker?" Hana asked.

"I do."

"Wow," she replied. "And I thought this couldn't get any crazier."

"I think it can always get crazier," Penelope added. "I know that from experience."

Marshall reached out for Penelope's hand and stroked the top of it with his thumb. He knew the story of her childhood. She'd shared it all.

"For how long?" Hana asked.

"I don't know," Marshall said. "I need to first see if Brian has the place and will let us stay there. But I'd wager that he does and he will. We'll go to him in person, assuming he'll let us in. We'll have to get out of here without being detected. We can't call him. We don't want anyone tracing our movements."

"That means we'll have to leave our phones. Or

destroy them," Penelope said, thinking out loud. "Hey, it works for me. Zach is the only real family I have. At least, he's the only one I keep in regular contact with. I don't mind going off grid for a while."

"Easy for you to say," Hana fussed. "I am close to my family. And my Instagram followers will wonder what happened to me."

Penelope did her best to stifle a laugh. Hana was a trust fund baby with too much time on her hands for her own good. She was focused on receiving attention, whether from her doting family or her adoring internet fans. She didn't even have a claim to fame. It wasn't like she was a musician, or a model. She was just a rich, attention seeking young woman who happened to be stunningly beautiful. Penelope had always wondered why Hana had even bothered with the escort business. She'd guessed for the glamorous lifestyle and attention from desperate men. Hana hadn't needed the money.

"I think your Instagram followers will survive," Penelope replied.

"She has a good point," Marshall said. "Depending on how long we're away, they might notice and raise red flags for police. Hana, can you schedule some posts right now to appear over the next few days?"

"Sure," Hana said. "You think this will all be over in a few days?"

"I can't say for sure, but it's a start."

Hana got busy on Instagram while Penelope asked more questions.

"What should I pack?"

"We need to pack light. We'll be leaving our vehicles,

and we don't know when or if we'll get another one. Think jump bag. Just the basics. How much cash do you keep on hand?"

Penelope was trying to keep up, but it all seemed surreal.

"I have cash," Hana said without looking up from her phone. "Nearly a thousand dollars. Will that be enough?"

"That should do it," Marshall answered.

"You have a thousand dollars in cash on you right now?" Penelope asked her friend. "I'd be surprised if I had a hundred. With debit and credit cards these days, I didn't think anyone carried a lot of cash."

"Yeah. So?" Hana replied.

"We may want to get more out of the ATM before we go into hiding," Marshall said. "Authorities may end up freezing our accounts at some point. And besides, we can't let them trace us."

"Luke and Neil seem nice," Penelope mused. "I can't imagine them going after us like that. They said they didn't think we had anything to do with Audrey's disappearance."

Marshall pulled Penelope to him and kissed her forehead. "Sweet Penelope, police aren't the only ones who might try to track us. That's why we're doing things the way we are. Bad guys-- as you call them-- are far more menacing than police."

"Right," Hana quipped. "Okay… and done!" She tossed her phone on the table. "Instagram posts have been scheduled for the next five days."

"That was fast," Marshall said.

"It's second nature."

The three of them leaned forward, expressing an unspoken agreement to get moving.

"We'll leave our phones here," Marshall instructed. "And our cars. Bring cash, a change of clothes, and anything we might use to disguise ourselves. Pack it in a small bag. Put on something comfortable and boring. We want to blend in."

"When do we go?" Penelope asked.

"Tonight. Once it gets dark, I'll make a test run out of the building to determine the best path. The three of us will leave after midnight. We'll go to Brian's house on foot. It's about eight miles from here, so wear walking shoes."

"Can't we get a car?" Hana asked.

Penelope couldn't help but laugh at how clueless and spoiled her friend was. "You want us to call an Uber? This is a small town, Hana. The idea is to move around undetected."

"Right," Hana said again. It was all she could think to say.

Turning her attention back to Marshall, Penelope squinted. "What happens when we get there?"

Marshall smiled. "We get busy. Brian will help us with traces of our own. I'm pretty sure this guy operates on the dark web. He's a programmer. I'll bet he can get us burner phones, contacts for resources and hire, and whatever else we need."

"It's like a real-life spy movie," Penelope added. "And I don't mean that in a bad way. If I have to be caught up in something like this, I'm just glad to have you by my side, Marshall, dear. You're like G.I. Joe. My own American Hero."

Marshall laughed. "I appreciate the vote of confidence. I'm not sure that's true, but I'll do my best for you. You know that."

Penelope *did* know that. She knew it for sure, the same way she'd known that her dad had loved and cherished her. It was just a shame that Felix hadn't been able to better protect her from Jean. Maybe Marshall would succeed in the protection department where Felix had fallen short. And maybe by doing so, it would help Penelope heal some fractured pieces from her rocky childhood. Felix had left her in harm's way, whether intentionally or not. But Marshall was here, physically by her side, ready to protect her. And he wasn't going anywhere.

A part of Penelope almost craved the danger, so that Marshall would have a chance to prove his allegiance and devotion. She knew it was messed up in many ways, but she wanted to feel whole. It had been hard to sort through the shambles of her own mental health and salvage the good. Coping mechanisms didn't always come easy.

"Oh, gag me now," Hana said.

She couldn't seem to help herself. Maybe she was jealous. Marshall and Penelope ignored her, sharing a quick kiss.

"But seriously," Hana raised. "What about Cheryl and Meg? They were at the party, too. And we know Cheryl saw something. I'll bet Meg did."

"She raises another good point," Marshall said.

Penelope seemed to agree. "Cheryl was here, not long before you arrived, Hana."

"Did she say anything about the party? Or Audrey?"

"No, but she seemed like she wanted to," Penelope explained. "She told me on the phone that she had something she wanted to talk about. Then when she was here, it seemed like she lost her nerve. I'm not sure what to make of it."

"Should we ask her?" Hana inquired. "If Cheryl was here not long before me, the blonde woman probably saw her. And since you already spoke to her on the phone, another call wouldn't seem odd, would it?"

Marshall lowered his brow, considering Hana's suggestion. "You raise another good point, Hana. How about you call Cheryl and get her back over here? We don't want loose ends floating around."

"I agree," Penelope said. "And Meg?"

"Do it," Marshall confirmed. "Get her here. If either Cheryl or Meg saw anything suspicious or know anything about what happened to Audrey, all five of us are going to Brian's together. Not only do we need to keep control of loose ends, we need to keep each other safe. I'd fear for Cheryl and Meg's safety if we didn't bring them with us."

"And Reggie?" Penelope asked. He was the last of the friend group and the head of the escort service. It was a question that had to be asked.

"We leave him be," Marshall replied. "He's not on our side."

13

———

By late evening, Marshall had done his test run and had found a way off the property that he was reasonably sure wouldn't be detected. He'd paid a boiler room attendant to help them gain safe passage out a narrow basement entrance. The blonde woman wouldn't be expecting them there. Penelope and Hana had packed a handful of jump bags, one for each member of their group. They assumed Cheryl and Meg would go willingly.

Penelope, Hana, and Marshall were eating dinner when they heard a knock at the front door. Cautiously, Marshall looked through the peephole, keeping one hand on his gun. It remained in his belt where he, no doubt, would keep it for the foreseeable future. Seeing Cheryl's face on the other side of the door, Marshall opened it just wide enough for the ladies to squeeze through. Both were dressed up, like they were going out to party. Marshall wondered if they shared Penelope's shoe size. He knew they'd never make it eight miles in the high heels they were wearing.

"Hey, Marshall," Cheryl said cheerfully. "Why the serious face?"

Penelope had asked Cheryl to come over and to bring Meg, but she hadn't told her why. Meg looked as beautiful as ever, but sober this time. It was a stark change from the previous morning on the dock.

"Are we here to celebrate the new couple?" Meg asked, grinning. "I hear we have lovebirds among us."

Penelope blushed. She couldn't help it. She hoped Hana didn't mention the scene she had walked in on. Penelope really didn't want them discussing her sex life.

Marshall smiled, though not too much. He was happy to be a couple with Penelope, but he knew he had work to do to protect her. There would be time to celebrate later.

"Sit down, will you?" Penelope asked, directing her friends to the dining table.

There were six seats at the table, the five of them almost filling her available space. Penelope hadn't envisioned serious, five-person discussions when she'd purchased the furniture. She made a mental note to get a bigger dining set when she and Marshall moved into their blue cottage in the country.

"You three look so serious," Meg commented, her curls bobbing as she plopped down in a chair.

"We have something important to discuss," Marshall said.

Meg and Cheryl looked at each other. They weren't used to having Marshall involved. It was usually just the four ladies. Marshall and Reggie had been friends of theirs, but not in their innermost circle. Group dynamics were changing.

"It's okay," Hana said, sensing Meg and Cheryl's concern. "He's good. You can talk openly in front of him."

Meg nodded. "Okay, then. So, how about you tell us what we're doing here."

Penelope gestured to Marshall. "You go ahead."

"Sure," Marshall said. "First, before we begin, will you please take your phone out, remove the batteries, and place them in the middle of the table?"

Cheryl gasped. "Whoa, whoa, whoa," she said. "Is that really necessary?"

"I'm afraid it is."

Penelope and Hana confirmed by nodding. They took their phones out and did as Marshall instructed.

Meg looked skeptical, but she shrugged and did as she was asked.

"Cheryl?" Marshall asked.

Cheryl didn't look convinced. At all. In fact, she looked like she might rebel against Marshall's leadership.

"What's the problem, Cheryl?" Hana asked, irritated. "Believe you me, I was skeptical, too. Before I understood what was happening."

"And what is happening?" Cheryl asked.

"We'll tell you all about it once you remove the battery on your phone and place it on the table," Marshall said as nicely as he could.

Marshall was a nice guy. A good guy. But he wasn't in the mood for delays. He and Penelope had already discussed this possibility privately, when Hana had gone to the bathroom. If Cheryl and Meg weren't cooperative, they'd leave them out of it. They couldn't afford to be hampered by someone who wasn't fully committed to getting through this alive. The stakes were life and death, even if it didn't seem like it. It was a fool's mistake to miss the signs and act careless. Marshall and Penelope wouldn't entertain such fools.

Cheryl stood, pulling a cigarette and a lighter out of her handbag and then lighting up. She walked towards one of the living room windows and looked out. Cheryl didn't usually smoke. Penelope hadn't known her to smoke more than a cigarette or two since college. Once when her cousin had overdosed, and once after a bad breakup.

"Cheryl, you're smoking?" Penelope asked.

"You don't need to make a big deal about it," Cheryl replied. "It helps me calm my nerves."

"Why do your nerves need calming?" Marshall asked. "Did you see what happened to Audrey?"

Hana stared down at the table. She knew she should let Penelope and Marshall handle this.

Cheryl coughed as a puff of smoke filled her lungs. "I don't have to tell you."

Marshall looked at Penelope, raising his eyebrows.

"Cheryl," Meg tried. "Don't be a bitch. Just tell them what you know and we can move on. It's not that big of a deal."

Apparently, Meg wasn't privy to anything that would indicate the gravity of the situation.

Cheryl coughed again and sputtered. She seemed stressed. More so than she had earlier in the day. Penelope was concerned about her.

There were a few moments of silence as they thought about their options. Hana tried to get through to Cheryl in the best way she knew how.

"Cheryl," Hana began. "Look out front there. On the sidewalk below. Or maybe across the street."

"Okay," Cheryl replied, peering out. "What am I looking for?"

"Do you see a blonde woman? Tall. Pretty mean looking. Seems like maybe she could be Russian or Eastern European."

Marshall took a deep breath as Cheryl scanned the scene before her. It took a minute.

"Oh!" Cheryl replied. "I see her. She's wearing all black, which seems out of place, now that you mention it. She has sharp features. She's sitting on the back of a motorcycle."

"That's her," Hana confirmed. "She's been following me since yesterday."

"What?" Meg asked, walking to the window to see for herself.

"You might as well wave," Hana said. "She knows that we see her. She's waiting for us, anyway."

Cheryl drew back, putting the cigarette out against the sole of her shoe.

"Hey!" Penelope said. "Watch the flooring, Cheryl. This isn't a nightclub."

"Sorry," Cheryl said, taking off her shoe then walking to the kitchen to clean it up with a paper towel.

Resigned to the inevitable conversation that needed to happen, Cheryl sat and took the battery out of her phone. She tossed it onto the table as Meg returned to the seat beside her. Both ladies looked spooked. Much of the color had drained from their faces.

"Good," Marshall said, resting his arms on the table and lacing his fingers together. "Before we tell you what we're planning, we'd like to hear whether you have information about Audrey's disappearance. You don't have to tell us what you know yet. Just whether you know something that the police or bad actors looking to cover up a crime might find valuable. Got it?"

Cheryl and Meg nodded, Cheryl reluctantly.

"Let's start with you, Meg," Marshall continued. "Did you see anything at the party the night Audrey went missing?"

Meg was bright eyed and seemed eager to help. Penelope was glad. She wished Meg had been so cooperative on the dock. Maybe they could have saved themselves some trouble.

"I didn't," Meg said. "Hand to God. I didn't see Audrey all night. Didn't even meet her."

"Where were you?" Marshall asked.

"I was wooing a potential client in the library," Meg explained. "Reggie had assigned me to him. His name was Dr. Mitch Bowker. A plastic surgeon from San Francisco. It was his first time at one of our parties. Reggie wanted me to convince him to hire our service and to bring some of his wealthy doctor friends with him next time."

"Were you his escort for the evening?" Marshall asked.

"No," Meg said. "Just doing the sales pitch. I had to sex it up and be alluring. But I wasn't actually on his service."

"And you were in the library with him all evening?" Penelope asked.

"That's right," Meg confirmed. "There was a jazz quartet in the library and Mitch was taken with them. Apparently, he played saxophone because he was telling me all about it. He was happy nursing his whisky and listening to the musicians play. We didn't see or hear anything about Audrey until first responders arrived and we went out back to find out what was going on."

Meg seemed believable. She didn't hesitate or show other telltale signs of lying. She didn't sip and sputter air like Penelope did.

"I swear," Meg added, meeting their eyes. "You can check the surveillance cameras."

Marshall looked at Penelope and Hana to let them know he was satisfied. "Good. Thank you, Meg."

"You're welcome, Marshall," she replied. "I hope that is helpful."

Meg seemed happy to defer to Marshall. She and Cheryl didn't know he'd been in the Marine Corps. Hana hadn't either until earlier in the day. But they could all tell that Marshall had something in his background that prepared him for a situation like this. Plus, he was a natural leader. The kind that leads by example instead of by force.

"It definitely is, Meg," Marshall replied. "I appreciate you sharing with us."

"Yes, thank you," Penelope echoed. Meg smiled and nodded, pleased.

The group took a collective breath as the focus shifted back to Cheryl. She wouldn't be as easy.

"Cheryl," Marshall began. "Now, you. Please?"

Cheryl grew agitated. She shook her knees under the table, thumping her heels against the floor. She caused such a vibration that Penelope grew concerned about her downstairs neighbors being disturbed. Penelope had never known Cheryl to be so fidgety. Something was bothering her, that was for sure.

"I don't know," Cheryl said. "I told the girls what I saw when the four of us were sitting on the dock yesterday morning. There was a handsome man who looked like Bradley Cooper, and I saw him eyeing Aubrey. That's all I saw, really."

"What did he look like, exactly?" Marshall asked.

"Like Bradley Cooper!" Cheryl practically yelled. "I don't remember anything else. How about you get off my back, would you?"

She pulled out another cigarette and prepared to light up until Penelope stopped her.

"Cheryl! No smoking in here," Penelope scolded.

"Sorry! Okay?"

Cheryl chewed her lip and continued to thump her legs as she put the cigarette back. All four of the others looked at each other now, growing suspicious.

"Cheryl," Marshall said gently yet firmly. "You seem scared. And we want to protect you if you're in danger. But we need to know that we're all on the same page here. You know? We need to know where our loyalties lie."

Cheryl shook her head. It seemed like she wanted to escape her current reality. The rest of them felt the same, but like Marshall had said, that isn't always possible. It wasn't in this circumstance.

Penelope reached across the table and took her friend's hand. She and Cheryl had been friends for so long, they were almost like sisters. She could see Cheryl suffering, and it hurt her heart.

"Cheryl, tell me," Penelope tried. "Whatever it is, we can handle it together. All five of us. Marshall will keep us safe."

Cheryl flew into a rage.

"Marshall? Marshall!" she yelled as she paced around the condo. "Why is Marshall suddenly in the middle of everything? Wasn't he just screwing Reggie— his husband who, by the way, runs the illegal escort service we all work for— a few days ago? And now he's some golden boy that we're all supposed to bow down to? Who died and made him king?"

"Wow," Hana muttered, placing a hand on her head. "That's a lot."

For his part, Marshall remained silent. He was thinking.

Tears welled in Penelope's eyes. Aside from her brother, Marshall and Cheryl were the two most important people in her life. The last thing she wanted was to see them pitted against each other.

"Cheryl, that was cruel. Please…" Penelope began.

"No, Pen," Cheryl continued, waving her hands in the air as she yelled. "It wasn't cruel. It's the only thing that's been said here tonight that's made an ounce of sense. I played the supportive friend when you told me about the two of you this afternoon, but this is too much. I can't be involved like this. I can't do it. I just… I can't…"

"He's a good guy, Cheryl," Penelope pleaded. "And

you don't know this, but he served in the Marines. He has experience that can help us."

"Oh, so I'm supposed to fall at his feet now and worship him? Because he served in the Marines? I don't think so. That means nothing to me."

Marshall stiffened. He didn't like to hear the Marine Corps disrespected like that. He took a deep breath, working to keep Cheryl's insults from getting to him. Hana shook her head and watched Cheryl and Penelope spar, while Meg stared at the table in front of her.

"That was rude," Penelope said.

"Was it?" Cheryl continued. "I think it was rude to bring him into our group and act as if he's suddenly our leader. We've all been friends for what? Fifteen years? And you and I have been friends much longer. You can't just bring someone in and expect us to put him up on a pedestal. It doesn't work like that, Pen."

"Cheryl," Marshall said softly. "You and I have known each other for quite some time. You know how Penelope and I have felt about each other. In fact, you know how I professed my love for her before Reggie and I ever got together. If Pen had told me how she really felt back then, I never would have…"

"Married Reggie? That's kind of a big slip up, don't you think?" Cheryl berated. "Like what? Did you just accidently fall and slip your dick in him? A man, for Christ's sake? And you want me to believe you really wanted Pen instead."

"Cheryl!" Penelope shouted. "You're taking this too far, and you're being rude."

"No, I deserve that," Marshall said. "You're right,

Cheryl. I should have tried harder with Pen. Or waited. Or… I don't know… The fact that Reggie is a man doesn't have anything to do with it."

Cheryl waved her hand in the air, dismissive. "Whatever." She reached for a cigarette again, then stopped. "Dammit!" she yelled.

Penelope stood, tears in her eyes. "Cheryl, I love you, but you need to leave. I won't let you talk to Marshall like that."

Cheryl scoffed. "Are you really choosing him over me? Your best friend? Your *oldest* friend?"

"I'm not choosing between you, but right now, I'm asking you to leave."

"Mark my words," Cheryl said, lowering her voice to a near whisper. "He's up to something. You shouldn't trust him."

Penelope closed her eyes and shook her head. She didn't want to hear it. And she didn't want Cheryl and Marshall to fight. "No."

"Oh, yes," Cheryl said, pointing in Marshall's direction. "He's no good for you. You'll see. If I were you, I'd take him back to his husband and wash your hands of the whole thing. If you don't, you'll be sorry."

14

As the front door slammed with Cheryl and Meg on the other side of it, Penelope burst into tears. Her friendships were important to her. Especially because she didn't have much family. She cherished her friendship with Cheryl most of all.

"Hey, now," Marshall said as he took Penelope into his embrace. "That was ugly. No doubt about it, but I don't think she meant the things she said, Pen."

Hana fretted in her chair, almost as upset as Penelope.

"I know Cheryl," Penelope replied, holding onto Marshall tightly. "That wasn't like her. It seemed like a completely different person talking. I just can't understand why she'd say those things about you."

"It's okay," Marshall said. "I'm not mad. I understand where she's coming from. She's protective of you, just like I am. If we can avoid being like two gladiators fighting against each other, I think she and I will find we have a lot in common."

Penelope sniffed and shook her head. "Maybe."

"Tensions are high right now," Marshall continued. "With Audrey missing and someone following Hana…"

"And they don't even know about the blonde man in the bay," Hana added. "Speaking of him, do dead bodies float to the surface? Or do they sink to the bottom?"

"Hana!" Penelope shouted.

"What? Sorry," Hana said. "I was just wondering. Never mind. I'll hush."

Penelope turned her attention back to Marshall. "I'm so hurt. You and Cheryl are more important to me than you know. I never dreamed that you'd quarrel with each other. Hell, it reminded me of being a child and listening to my parents argue."

"Oh?" Marshall asked. "I wasn't arguing, though, Pen. I was more trying to be rational and sane while Cheryl went off."

"Exactly what my dad used to say about my mom," Penelope added. "He was rational and sane while she went off, but that didn't spare us the drama and the stress. It was awful, just like tonight."

Marshall hugged her tighter, stroking her hair. "I'm sorry, Pen. I don't want that for you. What you went through with your mom sounds terrible. I certainly don't want to be part of anything that reminds you of that. What can I do?"

Penelope sobbed, her body heaving, full of repressed trauma that was coming to the surface. The pressure of her current situation had put her on edge. Then the dynamic between Cheryl and Marshall had triggered childhood memories she would rather forget. She was embarrassed to be crying like this in front of Hana. And she hated to be crying like this in front of Marshall, too. She was a grown woman in her mid-thirties. She should have been over her childhood trauma by now. She didn't want to seem insecure. She was afraid Marshall might not like her as much if she seemed delicate and clingy.

"I don't know," Penelope said. "I'm sorry."

"Hey," Marshall said, pushing Penelope's shoulders away from him so he could see her face. "You don't have anything to be sorry for. Don't say it."

"But…" Penelope had a hard time maintaining any composure.

"But nothing," Marshall said. "You're entitled to your feelings. I'm here for you. You cry all you want."

Penelope sobbed harder, unable to stop.

Feeling like she was intruding but having nowhere else to go, Hana excused herself and went into the bedroom to watch some TV. They weren't scheduled to leave until midnight, anyway. She figured she should give Penelope and Marshall some privacy.

Alone in the living room, Marshall guided Penelope to the sofa where she sprawled out across his lap. They talked quietly, about childhood and love, and about how hurts from the past could sneak up on even the best of us. Penelope was impressed by Marshall's tender care. His response to her breakdown was kind and healthy. He was solid. She could tell. It was at that moment she knew: Marshall was the man for her. The only one. So what if she was interested in him partially because he had many of the same positive qualities as her dad? That was a good thing. She knew that the two of them could build a happy life together... A healthy and *happy* life. She'd go to counseling if necessary to work out her issues. But she would be okay.

Marshall was her future.

"I choose you," Penelope said.

"Pen," he replied, "I choose you, too."

"I mean for the rest of my life. I choose you."

Marshall's face turned to an expression of complete happiness. A tear fell from his eye and landed on Penelope's forehead. He leaned down, wiping the tear away and then pulling her to him.

"Oh, Pen," he said softly. "You're my one and only. I choose you for the rest of my life, too. I'm sorry we got so far apart from each other before joining together. But we're together now. And that's the way we'll stay."

"You promise?"

"I promise," Marshall agreed. "I won't let anything tear us apart."

"Even the people following us? Because they seem pretty scary to me."

"Even the people following us. I'll protect you, Pen. With my life, if I have to. No one will hurt you as long as I walk this Earth."

Penelope hugged Marshall tightly and cried some more. She felt seen in a real, true way. This was it. She was beyond grateful to be the recipient of Marshall's love and affection. She'd known how good it could feel because she'd felt a similar love as a child, from Felix. Now, if she could just keep that kind of love in her life without the flip side of the coin. If she could keep the unconditional love without losing it, and without it being dampened by circumstances beyond her control. That remained to be seen.

15

____

The clock ticked toward midnight. Penelope, Marshall, and Hana closed the shades, locked up the condo, and made their way out of the building carrying nothing but their jump bags and Marshall's gun. They had left their phones on the dining table with the batteries out.

Penelope had debated leaving a note in case Zach came looking for her and used his key to enter her apartment, but Marshall advised her to skip it. It made sense. Any information that could inadvertently lead the blonde woman and her associates to them was a bad idea. There would be time to fill Zach in later. Penelope knew Zach was tough. That was a useful byproduct of growing up with a mother like Jean. And Zach knew that Penelope was tough, just the same. He'd be worried if he found out she was missing, but he'd know she could take good care of herself. She'd had a lifetime of practice.

The night air was cool as the threesome exited through the back door of the building. The wind was still, and the world was quiet. Most of the people of Rosemary Run were sleeping at this hour. The moon was bright and nearly full. It illuminated their surroundings. Marshall mentioned that complete darkness would have been better, but the soft light of the moon provided a small comfort to Penelope and Hana. They weren't ashamed to admit it: they were scared. If it weren't for Marshall being there to physically protect them, they weren't sure what they would have done. Neither felt strong enough to fight their way out of danger with their hands alone. If Marshall hadn't been there when the blonde man had approached with the gun, the situation would have surely turned out quite differently.

The blonde woman out front had been at her post and sitting on her motorcycle, the last glimpse Penelope had gotten of her as she pulled the shades shut. She hoped to God that the woman would stay put long enough for them to get off the property and on their way. She also hoped that the woman didn't have a colleague who was watching the back. It was all so strange. Penelope couldn't begin to understand it. But she was determined to get through alive. She wasn't ready for her life to end. Not when it was just getting started.

"Keep your steps soft," Marshall whispered. "Stay close to me."

They were wearing all black and slinking around like cat burglars. Marshall led the way, followed by Penelope, then Hana.

"Okay," Hana said loudly from the back.

"Shh," Penelope hushed. "That was loud, Hana. Be quieter."

"Okay," Hana tried again, in a whisper this time.

Penelope thought of the absurdity of it all as they cleared the parking lot and made their way south down a side street. Here they were, walking for miles in the middle of the night, going to a man's house without advance notice, and expecting to be welcomed into a doomsday bunker where they'd set up a base of operations to lure whatever assassins were after them and collect evidence for the police. Or something like that. Maybe she had the steps out of order. Or maybe she was missing steps. At any rate, their current truth was stranger than fiction. Even though she was mad at Cheryl, Penelope could understand how ridiculous this looked. And Cheryl didn't even hear this part of the story. She didn't even know about the blonde man in the bay. She would probably have gone even more berserk if she had known.

"Quick," Marshall said as a pair of headlights appeared in the distance. "Over here."

The ladies followed his lead, stepping into a dark alley and pressing themselves up against a concrete wall. They watched as the vehicle drove slowly past, oblivious to their presence. So far, so good. They were undetected.

"Okay, clear," Marshall called. "It will be easier once we get out of the densely populated part of town. A few more miles and there won't be many cars going by."

They stepped back onto the street and hurried, hugging the curb.

"Can we talk now?" Hana asked. "It would help me relax. I'm a bundle of nerves."

"Let's wait awhile longer," Marshall replied. "At least

until we get a little farther. Keep your eyes peeled for other people. Focus on that. We don't want to be seen."

"Okay," Hana said. She inhaled deeply.

"Good going, Hana," Penelope offered. "We'll get through this."

"Hey," Hana tried. "Can I hum?"

Marshall turned and looked back at her, frustrated. "The idea is to get to Brian's without being seen. And being heard might lead to being seen. You know? Let's be quiet. Please."

Hana sighed. "Okay."

A few moments passed as they walked in silence.

"Should we run?" Hana asked.

Marshall and Penelope thought Hana was just nervous again, and asking about things that would help her cope.

"Shh," Penelope said, motioning with one hand.

"I mean it. Guys? Should we run?"

Penelope and Marshall turned and saw a dog rushing towards them. It wasn't barking— thank God— but it was moving fast, panting with exertion. Penelope couldn't tell for sure, but it looked like a German Shepherd. It was big. And dark. She could barely make out its coloring. It looked menacing.

"Oh, shit!" Marshall exclaimed.

"What do we do?" Penelope asked.

They were still walking, but the terror coursing throughout their bodies beckoned them to run, just as Hana had suggested.

"I think this is a trained attack dog. Someone sent it after us," Marshall said.

Hearing his words, Penelope and Hana froze. Marshall stopped, then turned to face the beast.

"Keep going," Marshall said without taking his eyes off the dog. "I told you Brian's address. Do you remember it?"

"But…" Penelope mumbled.

"No time, Pen. Do you remember the address?"

"Yes!" Hana screamed. "I remember it."

"Then go there. Run. Right now. Tell him who you are to me. I'll catch up to you as soon as I can."

"Marshall, I won't leave you," Penelope said, bursting into tears. "I can't…"

"Penelope, GO!" Marshall yelled. "Go, now!"

Hana pulled on her friend's arm, ushering her away. Penelope screamed, filling the night with sound. But she did as Marshall instructed. She ran. She turned her back to him and, along with Hana, ran as fast as she could south out of town. They heard the sickening thud as the dog made impact with Marshall's body, but they didn't look back.

Terror had descended upon them. Like victims in a horror movie, Penelope and Hana feared the unseen and the unknown. They were afraid to look back and afraid to look ahead. They weren't sure how they would make it the eight miles to Brian's house without being taken down by whoever was chasing them. And that was just the first of many uncertainties. They didn't know if Brian would let them in when they arrived. What if he didn't believe them? What if he didn't care?

They ran. And they ran. They didn't speak. They just ran.

Hana led the way, showing a surprising knack for remembering what Marshall had said and following his directions. They made it to Brian's house on the outskirts of town without so much as one wrong turn. Their legs felt like jelly when they arrived, but thanks to adrenaline, their limbs had not failed them.

They walked up to the front door and rang the bell.

16

Brian's house was unassuming. It was a small country cottage, much like the one Penelope had envisioned her and Marshall growing old in. It sat on a large plot of land with what looked like a garden that had recently been planted around one side. Penelope and Hana could see from the front porch that the soil had been freshly tilled. The smell of manure wafted through the air. It must have been laid down as fertilizer for the growing seeds.

There was an old Ford pickup truck in the driveway. Probably a seventies model. Red with horizontal white stripes down both sides. Penelope wasn't much of a car buff, but it reminded her of a truck Felix had when she was a kid. A windsock rippled with a light breeze.

A child's tricycle sat on one side of the driveway near the barn. It looked relatively new and had sparkly streamers hanging from each handlebar. A little girl. Brian had a little girl. A quick scan of the property told Penelope that this little girl was well cared for. A tire swing hung in a large tree in the front yard. And a chalk drawing had recently been added to the front walk. Penelope estimated that she was three or four, based on her interests.

Penelope had good memories of her own from ages three and four. Jean had been more stable at that time, flush with a support system of extended family and friends. Perhaps Jean's mental illness hadn't yet reared its ugly head. Or perhaps Jean could better deal with a child too young to have opinions that contradicted her own. Either way, Penelope looked back on that age and remembered happy times.

"Look," Penelope said to Hana, gesturing with her head. "He has a child."

Hana looked around as they waited for someone to come to the door. "That means he'll be more protective," Hana replied. "He'll want to keep her safe."

"You're right," Penelope agreed. "Let's hope he doesn't shoot us dead on the spot. Wouldn't you? If someone came to your country house in the middle of the night asking you to take them in because assassins were after them and your Marine Corps buddy told you to take refuge here?"

"It's a lot," Hana agreed.

"You can say that again."

When a few minutes had passed and no one came, Penelope knocked. "Maybe the bell is busted."

They waited another few minutes, periodically glancing over their shoulders and hoping no one would find them here. Except Marshall, of course. They would have both liked to see him walk up the driveway and reassure them everything was okay.

"Maybe it's the wrong house," Penelope tried. "Tell me again the address Marshall gave us?"

"This is it," Hana replied. "1532 Morningbell Lane. It's a Rosemary Run address, even though it's outside the city limits."

"That's what I remember, too," Penelope said. "And it's right there on the mailbox out by the road: 1532 Morningbell Lane. This is Brian's house."

"Unless he moved or something," Hana said. "Maybe Marshall lost touch."

"I don't know," Penelope said, shoving her hands into her pockets to warm them. Temperatures had dropped overnight. It was cool. "It seems like a guy who goes to the trouble of building an underground bunker wouldn't up and leave it."

"Right?" Hana asked.

Finally, they heard movement inside the house. Someone was up.

"Here we go," Penelope said. "Let's hope this doesn't go sideways. We're running out of options. And fast."

The door handle jingled as if there were bells on the inside. Heavy footsteps shuffled. A light turned on, and as it did, it illuminated a U.S. Marine Corps decal affixed to the front door just above the handle. It had been hard to see before due to a screen. The wooden door creaked as it opened, finally revealing a face that reminded Penelope of Marshall's.

"That's got to be him," she whispered to Hana.
Hana nodded.
"Hello? Brian Patterson?" Penelope asked.

"Who wants to know?" the man replied, keeping one hand hidden behind the door.

"I told you," Penelope whispered to Hana. "He probably has a gun behind the door. And we're unarmed."

The man looked at them hard, suspicious of their whispering. Penelope told herself to get it together.

"Um, I know this is crazy… It's the middle of the night and all…"

"Just get to the point," the man said. "Where did you get that name?"

"Brian?" Penelope asked.

Hana elbowed her and gave her a look that said to get on with it.

The man nodded, then sort of grunted. He seemed rougher than Marshall.

"Right," Penelope continued, trying to focus. "Marshall Erving. Our friend… my boyfriend…"

"Marshall?" the man said, his voice noticeably softening.

"Yes. Marshall told us to come to you. He was with us, but a dog chased him. It's a long story."

"Marshall Erving told you to come here? To me?"

"Yes," Penelope confirmed. "He said you two served in Iraq together and that you had an underground bunker where we'd be…"

The man opened the screen door and pulled Penelope and Hana inside with one hand, carefully looking around outside to make sure no one was watching. As Penelope expected, he had a rifle in his other hand.

"Come in," he said.

He gestured to a leather sofa in front of a fireplace,

then bolted up the front door behind them. Penelope counted six deadbolts and two chains. She'd never seen anyone so well protected or prepared. She wasn't sure what to make of it. Hana apparently felt the same way. Her eyes were wide. She was sitting on her hands, probably to keep from chewing on what was left of her fingernails.

The man sat in a recliner across from them, letting the rifle rest across his lap. Penelope wasn't very knowledgeable about guns, but she thought she recognized the clip, inserted into the weapon and ready to go.

"I'm Brian Patterson," he confirmed, taking a wad of chewing tobacco out of a metal container and tucking it under his bottom lip. "What the hell are you two doing out here? And tell me the whole story, beginning to end."

Penelope began explaining how long she'd known Marshall and how she didn't requite his feelings, leading him to marry Reggie.

"Marshall Erving? Married to a man?" Brian asked, genuinely surprised.

"Yes," Penelope replied.

"Huh," Brian said. "Okay, then."

She continued with the story of the escort service and how Marshall had gotten wrapped up in it with Reggie. She told him about her and Hana's jobs that included recruiting young girls and entertaining prospective clients, especially those who would tell their wealthy friends.

"So you're high dollar prostitutes?" Brian asked.

He focused his attention on Penelope as she was talking, but his eyes repeatedly wandered to Hana. He was taken by her striking beauty, Penelope could tell. She wondered if Brian had a wife or a girlfriend. The little girl had a mother somewhere, or at least, at some point. Penelope didn't immediately see evidence of a woman in the house. It looked like a man had done the decorating. It was all masculine, with little girl toys here and there.

Penelope thought maybe she should let Hana do the talking. If Hana's looks could help them now, then Penelope was all for using that to their advantage. They needed all the help they could get.

"No," Hana blurted, sensing Brian's interest in her. "We don't sleep with the men and we are definitely not prostitutes. And we're getting out of it, anyway."

If Penelope didn't know better, she thought Hana was showing interest in Brian, too. She was sitting up straight, her back arched seductively. She crossed one leg over the other in a feminine pose.

"I see," Brian said. "Just asking. That's all. I don't mean any offense."

Hana picked up where Penelope had left off. Marshall had said they'd tell Brian everything, so the ladies felt compelled to do so. The details might be important to Brian, if he agreed to help them.

Hana explained about Audrey and the men who had drugged her then let her slide underwater in the pool. She told Brian about the next morning and the blonde man she'd seen hiding in the hedges at Reggie's house, and how he'd approached them on the dock while holding Reggie at gunpoint. Brian's eyebrows rose as he listened. He seemed like a pretty stoic guy, but he was surprised. He nearly rose out of his chair when Hana told him how the blonde man had wanted to take her.

"He had a gun on you?" Brian asked with a protective tone.

Penelope saw the smile that began to form at the edge of Hana's lips. She liked this guy. Who would have thought? They seemed like an odd pair, but opposites often do attract.

"He did," Hana said. "It was scary. I hid behind Marshall."

"That's my guy," Brian said. "Good dude, that Marshall Erving."

Penelope and Hana nodded their agreement. "The best," Penelope said softly.

Hana continued the story, explaining how Marshall and then Penelope had wrestled with the blonde man, eventually choking him and letting his lifeless body drop into the bay.

"It was intense," Hana concluded.

"Sounds like it," Brian said. "But how did you get here? Did you walk?"

"Yes. Well, more like we ran," Hana said. She explained the rest: the blonde woman, Marshall's plan, the German Shepherd. "And here we are."

"So, you're telling me Marshall got snarled up with an attack dog? And you don't know where he is right now?"

"That's right," Penelope said. "He told us to keep going and to find you. He said he'd catch up to us as soon as he could."

Brian stood and carefully looked out the windows. He seemed to be debating what to do. Penelope and Hana could tell he was a good guy, just like Marshall had said. Brian was a protector. It almost seemed like he wanted to go look for Marshall. When his eyes left the windows, they moved to an interior hallway. His little girl was probably asleep there in her bedroom.

"You have a child?" Hana asked.

Brian sat back down in the chair. Same pose, with his rifle resting on his lap.

"I do. A girl. Madeline. She's four."

"Aw," Penelope said. "How sweet."

She often dreamed of a little girl. She'd tried to push the thought out of her mind. She wasn't even coupled until yesterday, let alone married. But visions of a little girl had occupied her mind, along with the blue cottage and big yard and puppies. Penelope and Marshall's girl would be smart. And pretty. She'd have brown hair like the both of them, and long limbs like Penelope. Most importantly, she'd be loved and cherished. Not just when she was little, but for her whole life. She'd be loved unconditionally. She would never be yelled at or ridiculed the way Penelope had. They'd break the cycle. Whatever it took.

Not a soul in the whole wide world knew it, but in the back of Penelope's bedroom closet, she had a bag filled with three little-girl outfits she'd purchased. One was a footed onesie for a newborn. It was pastel pink with small green and white flowers. It zipped up the front. Another was a summer sundress that was perfect for a first birthday celebration. It had big blue and purple flowers, with a bow on the front. The third item was a matched set of pants and a top for a toddler. The pants were blue and the top was pink and purple, colors that Penelope had always liked. They were colors that her mother had often dressed her in. Before Jean had turned mean and unforgiving.

"She's the light of my life," Brian said, smiling a huge grin. His face changed when he talked about her.

"That's so nice," Hana said, smiling back at him.

Penelope had never known Hana to be interested in kids, but she seemed sincere now.

"Where's her mom?" Penelope asked.

Hana elbowed her. "Pen!"

Brian chuckled. "It's okay. I just learned a hell of a lot about you two. I can answer a few questions about myself."

Hana smiled, clearly pleased that she would learn Brian's relationship status.

"Madeline's mom passed away not long after she was born," Brian explained. "Ovarian cancer. We didn't know she had it until it was too late."

"Oh," Hana said, raising a hand to her mouth. "I'm so sorry."

"Yeah," Brian continued. "Symptoms of that disease don't usually show up until it's pretty advanced anyway, and the pregnancy hid it even more."

"That's terrible," Penelope offered.

"It's okay," Brian said. "In life, you win some and you lose some. And you know what?"

"What?" Hana asked eagerly.

"If we'd known Jessa was sick, we never would have gotten pregnant. And we wouldn't have brought our precious Madeline into the world. Everything happened the way it had to. Jessa gave me the greatest gift I've ever received. I'll be eternally grateful."

He wiped a tear from his eyes and pressed his lips together, trying to maintain his composure.

"Wow," Hana said. "That's amazing. You're amazing."

Penelope looked at her friend, wanting to elbow her back.

"What?" Hana asked. "It is. He is!"

"Why, thank you," Brian said, smiling.

They had only been inside his house for half an hour, but it felt like they were old friends. And it felt like Brian and Hana might end up much more. When the conversation lulled and thoughts turned back to the matter at hand, Brian leaned forward, placing his rifle down on the floor beside him.

"I'm going to show you something," he began. "But I don't want you to tell anyone what you'll see here. Do you understand?"

"Is it your bunker?" Hana asked. "Marshall told us you were building one."

"Yes," Brian said. "It's fully functional now. But I'm serious. Not a word about what you will see here. Ever. Do you understand? Tell me you understand."

"I understand," Penelope replied.

"Me, too. I understand," Hana said.

"Okay," Brain said, standing. "Come with me."

17

Brian went to Madeline's room and gently lifted her out of bed on the way to the basement. He placed her against his shoulder and gently wrapped her blanket around her.

"Shh," he said. "Daddy's got you. Go back to sleep."

The girl stirred only a little, then settled into a peaceful slumber on her dad's shoulder. She trusted him completely.

Penelope and Hana waited in the hall. When Brian arrived with Madeline on his shoulder, their hearts practically melted. Madeline was a beautiful little girl with dark hair, chubby cheeks, and the sweetest pink lips. She almost looked like she could be Hana's child, which was a bit of a surprise, because Brian was much lighter complected.

"She's the sweetest," Hana said, instinctively reaching to touch the child's leg. Brian smiled. He didn't mind. In fact, it appeared that magic was happening right before their eyes.

"Thank you," Brian said. "I think so. Now, Hana, grab my rifle. And follow me."

He led them down a set of narrow stairs into what looked like a run-of-the-mill basement. Hana carried the rifle dutifully. At the bottom of the stairs, Brian pulled a string that turned on a single light bulb, careful to cover Madeline's eyes. Once the room was lit, Penelope and Hana could see row after row of canned food on dusty shelves. It looked like enough to feed a family for months, if not years.

"Is this a canning cellar?" Hana asked, seeming taken with the whole lifestyle. Penelope doubted her friend had ever seen such a thing in person before. She doubted she'd held a rifle before either.

"Indeed, it is," Brian said. "My grandparents taught me. I like to be prepared."

"Prepared for what?" Penelope asked.

Brian chuckled.

Hana elbowed Penelope again, then continued, awestruck, "Did you grow all of this food in your garden?"

"There. And on my trees," Brian answered.

"You are amazing," Hana said quietly. She sounded like a smitten teenager.

Penelope continued to marvel at the vibes happening between Hana and Brian. She would not have predicted this pairing. But then again, who was she to predict anything? She was the one who had gotten together with Marshall against all odds. At least, that's the way it probably seemed.

Penelope missed Marshall terribly, and she was worried about him. "Say, Brian," she began. "I don't mean to interrupt the tour, but do you think Marshall is okay? I'm afraid something bad might happen. I don't know what I'd do without him."

Brian smiled sympathetically. He had a kind face, although he could look fierce when he needed to. The ladies had learned that when he'd answered the door.

"I don't know," Brian said. "It sounds like you three have a real debacle on your hands. A dangerous one, at that. But if I know anything about Marshall, it's that he perseveres. When we were under fire in Iraq, there was no one else I would have rather had by my side. If anyone can make it through and get here safely, to you, it's Marshall."

Hana sighed. It seemed like she had a new appreciation for Marshall and others like him. Like his friend, Brian. "Oh, Pen," she said, putting an arm around Penelope. "I think he'll make it here. He has to."

Appeased for the moment, Penelope nodded and the tour continued. She did her best to say strong.

At the back of the canning cellar, Brian placed his hand on a sturdy workbench. Using the free hand, he scooted it out from the wall about an inch, exposing a metal lever. Slowly, he pulled the lever. As he did, a six-foot section of the wall beyond moved. The wall-door slid sideways, opening to a metal elevator shaft that looked like it belonged in a factory, not a basement. A large elevator cage sat at the ready. It looked large enough to transport big pieces of equipment. And lots of people.

"This is next level," Hana said, quietly so as not to disturb Madeline. "You're one of those doomsday preppers, aren't you?"

Brian shrugged. "I don't know. I might fit in that category. Like I said, I like to be prepared."

He pulled the workbench back into its place, careful to obscure the view of the button in case someone came down the stairs. Inside the elevator, he pushed another button and the door slid closed. A mechanical whirr sounded, and they descended. Brian placed a hand gently over Madeline's ear so she wouldn't be woken up by the noise.

"Hold on," he said, gesturing to the rail.

"How low are we going?" Penelope asked.

"The equivalent of two stories down, which is three total if you count the basement as one below the main level."

"Amazing," Hana said, beginning to sound like a broken record. "Madeline doesn't wake up?"

"Nah," Brian said. "Not usually. She's used to me moving her from the truck to the bed after she falls asleep while we're riding. And we come down here sometimes. She feels safe with her daddy."

Penelope and Hana nearly choked up. It was so nice. Brian was so nice. And Marshall was nice, too. The ladies could see why Marshall and Brian were friends.

When the elevator stopped at the bottom of the shaft, Brian pushed the button again, and the door opened. If Penelope and Hana had been impressed before, the sight before them took their admiration of Brian to a whole new level.

There, under Brian's unassuming country cottage, was a high-tech bunker like something you might see in a movie. Penelope and Hana's jaws hung open. It was remarkable.

As they looked around, they saw a full kitchen with stainless steel counters, appliances, and shelves. Potted plants were situated on the floors and grew tall, all the way up to shoulder height. It looked like the plants were lettuce and other edibles. There was a living room area with several sleek daybeds that looked like they'd do double duty as sofas and sleeping quarters. All the decor was sleek and modern. But that wasn't all. The tech was incredible. Monitors and screens took up an entire room in the back. Brian had his own server and four workstations in that room alone. Next to the tech room were three bedrooms with bunk beds. A total of twelve bunks sat available, ready for use. Each bedroom had a computer workstation as well. Last but not least, there was a huge storage room off the kitchen.

"What's back there?" Hana asked.

"Go on in," Brian replied. "You'll see."

Nonperishable food lined the walls. Stacks and stacks of it. A rack in the back held guns. Lots of them. And bulletproof armor.

"Brian, this is…" Hana continued.

"This place can keep fifteen people alive underground for up to two years, depending on how much we all eat. Eighteen people in a pinch."

Penelope had heard about people who prepped like this, but she didn't know details of what they included. She certainly hadn't seen anything like this in person. Most of the people she knew didn't plan their entire week of groceries, let alone how fifteen people— eighteen in a pinch— could survive in a bunker for a couple of years. She was speechless. Marshall had sent them to the right place, that was for sure. There was no way the blonde woman and her buddies could get them down here.

Hana seemed to be weirdly aroused by all of this. She stood close to Brian and licked her lips while staring at his mouth. It looked like she wanted an excuse to touch him.

"Do you have a private room down here?" Hana asked, her voice now a purr.

Brian smiled. He was feeling it. "I do. Last one on the right."

"And Madeline?"

"She usually sticks with me when we hang out down here, but she has her own space. It's a smaller room connected to my bedroom. I can lay her in there if she's playing quietly. Or sleeping."

"Can you show me?" Hana asked, the pheromones flying.

Penelope suddenly felt like a third— or would that be fourth?— wheel. She blushed, but remembered that Hana had walked in on her and Marshall earlier when Penelope's legs had been spread wide open, Marshall's face buried in between. Penelope guessed they were beyond being ashamed of such things.

"Say," Penelope offered. "I'm feeling tired and would love a short nap if there's time. Maybe Madeline and I could settle into one of the bunks? I'll look after her. Then you two can continue the tour."

Hana looked at her friend and mouthed the words thank you. Brian smiled. He patted Madeline's back, thinking. He glanced at the door to the elevator, then went to double check the lock. It was pressure sealed from inside. He walked to the main station in the tech room and flipped on the monitors. Cameras from around his property fed into the station and provided a three-sixty view. All was quiet.

"Okay, Penelope," he said. "I appreciate you looking after my baby girl while you nap. I'd enjoy the chance to show Hana around some more. Here, you can take this room." Brian gestured to the first bunk room, then laid Madeline down on one of the bottom bunks. She barely stirred. "She should stay sleeping. She's comfortable down here. You take the bunk directly across from her. If she wakes up, just tell her you're a friend of mine and that I'll be right back."

"Got it," Penelope replied.

"Oh, and if she asks, the code word is pineapple pancakes."

"Okay," Penelope said. "Got that, too. You are one prepared man."

Brian shrugged and smiled as he tucked his daughter in, pulling her little blanket up over her shoulders. "It's just the way I am."

Hana beamed, her excitement overflowing. She and Brian exited the room, closing the door behind them.

Penelope did need to rest. That wasn't a lie. Besides, she would have been sipping air and holding her breath if it had been. She couldn't stop her body from doing that melodramatic bit, even for a little white lie, unfortunately. She wondered if she'd ever outgrow that particular condition. Figuring it didn't matter, she closed her eyes. She felt safe. Marshall stayed on her mind, but she knew there wasn't anything she could do to help him right now. Hopefully, he'd be there soon. If he was there, he'd tell her to get some rest. She glanced at Madeline to make sure the girl was still sleeping soundly, then she joined her, drifting off to sleep.

18

When Penelope woke, she noticed that Madeline was no longer in the room. She jumped out of her bunk, her mind reeling. Being underground, it was impossible to tell what time of day it was or how long she'd been sleeping. Penelope typically used her phone to keep up with times and alarms, but she didn't have that, either. She needed to get a burner phone soon, before she lost complete track.

"Madeline? Brian?" she called, rubbing her eyes. "Hana?"

It felt to Penelope like she'd been sleeping less than an hour, but she suspected it had been much longer. She hoped Madeline was safe. So much for looking after the girl.

"Out here!" Hana called, cheerfully, from the main room.

"Coming," Penelope replied.

She stood, then tousled her hair with her fingers,

attempting to look decent. She needed a shower. Those eight miles had left her disheveled and sticky.

When she walked out of the bunk room to join the others, she saw quite a happy scene. Brian was seated on one of the sofa beds with his arms stretched out along the back. He looked satisfied. Hana sat beside him, one hand on his knee while she used the other to play dolls with little Madeline. For her part, Madeline smiled sweetly, enamored with Hana. They looked like a family.

"That was fast," Penelope said, before she had a chance to think better of it. "How long was I out?"

"Pen!" Hana said softly, opening her eyes wide and tilting her head. "Stop it."

Penelope shook her head. "Sorry. I didn't mean it like that. Let me try again… Good morning."

"Good morning to you, too," Brian said. "Penelope, meet Miss Madeline."

"Hi, Penewlope," Madeline said, the mispronunciation adorable. Penelope is a hard name for a little kid to say.

"Hi, there," Penelope replied, sitting down on another sofa bed nearby. "You can call me Pen, if you want. All of my friends do. Are these your dolls?"

Madeline smiled. "Pen. Okie dokie." Then she launched into an explanation of who the dolls were and what they were doing. She had four total. Sisters, she said.

Something about the dolls reminded Penelope of her friends. A pang of sadness hit her. The four of them had been close for so long that it seemed troublesome for them to be at odds like this. "You know what?" Penelope asked.

"What?" Madeline replied. She was such a cutie.

"I have three friends and together, there are four of us.

Just like your dolls. We've been friends for a long time. Hana is one of us, too."

Madeline looked over at Hana and back at Penelope. "Where are your friends?" she asked innocently.

Hana sighed. She felt sad, too.

"I'm not sure where the other two are right now," Penelope explained. "But Hana and I are here. I'm sure we'll see the others soon."

Hana stood, changing the subject. "Pen, how about some coffee? Brian made us some."

"Sure. And, seriously, how long was I out?"

Brian looked at the smartwatch on his arm. "About five hours," he said.

"Five hours? Wow," Penelope mused. "It felt like one hour. Maybe two. I guess our little run last night wore me out."

Brian chuckled.

"Have you heard from Marshall?" Penelope added.

"No, nothing yet," Brian replied. "All has been quiet around here. But I'm ready to get to work on your… situation… once you've had coffee and something to eat. There's a shower if you want one."

"Great. Thanks," Penelope said.

Brian had made them some eggs and pancakes, complete with pineapple topping. Apparently, there was a good reason for using pineapple pancakes as a code word. Penelope ate like she was starving, filling her belly with more food than she thought she could hold. She figured the stress was probably affecting her. When she was finished eating, she showered then changed into a clean set of clothes from her go bag. Hana and Brian had already changed, so Penelope assumed they had showered, too.

She wanted to ask Hana what was happening with her and Brian, but she decided to be mature about it and wait. There were more pressing matters at hand. And besides, it was plain to see what was happening between them, really. Regardless of whether or not they'd had sex last night, they were very much a couple. And a happy one, at that. Stranger things had happened.

Ready to move forward and face whatever the day might bring, Penelope joined Brian and Hana in the tech room. Madeline continued to play with her dolls in the main living area nearby. Brian had three of the monitors turned on and was searching through the day's news when Penelope arrived.

"I'm here," Penelope said, plopping down in a squishy chair. She had to give Brian credit. The place was as comfortable as it was functional. He had done an amazing job. "Great place, by the way, Brian. You should design these things for VIPs. You know, like the president and cabinet members. Maybe military leaders. Don't they have bunkers like this, only bigger?"

Brian chuckled, then glanced at Hana. "Something like that."

Penelope was surprised that the two of them already had inside jokes and shared information. But okay. Maybe they had stayed up talking while she slept.

"Ready to get started?" Brian asked.

"Affirmative," Penelope said, feeling official. It seemed like the right vine under the circumstances. "What are we looking for? What's the plan?"

"Well, we'll start with the news," Brian explained. "Local, then regional, then national, then international."

"Yikes," Penelope said. "International, even?"

"We'll want to cover all the bases. Depending on what we find, I'll dig deeper."

"You mean on the dark web?" Penelope asked.

"Maybe, if it will help."

Hana smiled proudly. She was enamored with Brian and living in her own real-life spy movie. Penelope understood because she felt much the same way about Marshall.

"And what will we do with the information we find?" Penelope asked. "Will we leave the bunker?"

"That remains to be seen," Brian replied. "For the moment, we'll stay put. I have contacts who can do the heavy lifting for us if that's needed. But yeah, maybe we'll go out and do some recon. It all depends on what we're dealing with here."

Penelope nodded. She liked being told what would happen. She had appreciated Marshall telling them his plans the night before. And it was a good thing he had. They wouldn't have known where to find Brian otherwise.

"Will people know we're missing?" Penelope asked. "Shouldn't you be tending to your garden?"

"You do like to know everything, don't you?" Brian asked.

Hana chucked. "You have no idea."

Now it was Penelope's turn to elbow Hana. "Hey now," she said to her friend.

They all laughed together. It felt good to take the pressure off for a moment.

"Yes, Penelope," Brian said. "I'll tend my garden. Don't worry about the details right now. Let's take this one step at a time. I'll fill you in as much as possible as we go along."

"Okay. Thank you," Penelope replied. "I guess I never knew what was coming next as a kid, so I've tried to avoid that same helpless feeling as an adult."

Brain nodded knowingly. "I get that. It's no problem. I'll keep you informed when I can. Here, you can help me out by taking a look at the morning newscast for Channel 2 out of Sacramento. Use that workstation in front of you. There are headphones in the drawer."

"Got it," Penelope replied.

"Hana," Brian said, her name causing his face to light up, "you take a look at Channel 5. I'll read through the local paper."

"Okay," Hana said. "Is Madeline okay out there alone?"

"She's fine for the moment," he confirmed. "I'll keep an eye on her. Once she's finished with dolls, I have a stack of coloring books and a new package of crayons ready."

"Oh, I always loved a new pack of crayons," Penelope chimed in. "One of childhood's simple pleasures."

Brain smiled. "We try to keep simple pleasures flowing around here."

For some reason, that made Hana blush, her cheeks flaring into a rosy pink brighter than Penelope had ever seen. Hana stuck her tongue out at her friend, teasing. "Hush," she said.

Penelope and Hana pulled out their headphones and placed them firmly over their ears. They were the big kind that fit like earmuffs. They were noise cancelling, too. They each navigated to the website of their assigned news station, while Brian pulled up the website for the Rosemary Run Journal. They settled in for what they figured would be a long and tedious process.

To Penelope's great surprise, Marshall's face greeted her when she landed on Channel 2's homepage. "Oh, my God," she said, both hands shooting up to cover her mouth.

"What is it?" Brian asked.

"It's here, too," Hana added. She hadn't heard Penelope through the headphones, but she had seen her reaction. She pulled one ear piece back so that she could converse. "It's Marshall. He's the top story."

They gathered around Penelope's monitor to watch the Channel 2 piece first. The headline told the story: *Human remains found in Sweet Balm Bay. Rosemary Run man charged.*

19

The day young Penelope had arrived home from the bank with the eighty-seven dollars from her savings account tucked into her pants pocket, her first of a series of difficult tasks had been to dispose of the small white envelope the cash had come in.

Penelope had never made such a withdrawal before-- she was nine-years-old, after all-- and she hadn't expected the envelope to be a part of the equation. If she had thought ahead or had done some research, she might have anticipated the need to dispose of it. She kicked herself for the oversight.

Jean didn't allow her daughter much privacy. Penelope knew she couldn't simply put the envelope in the household trash. So she'd had to scheme. And the envelope was just the beginning. It was a shame, really. Penelope hadn't wanted to sneak around. She hadn't seen any other way. In fact, Felix, of all people, had shown her that hiding things from Jean had been necessary.

Six months prior to the Sunnyday Sales Club ordeal

and the savings account withdrawal, Felix had told Penelope that he'd planned to get her a ten-speed bike for her upcoming birthday. She'd wanted one like it for what felt to a young girl like forever. She wanted it to be blue, with a soft seat and gears on the long handlebars that snaked downwards, designed for a good grip while leaning forward to ride fast.

The bike had seemed out of reach, a luxury Penelope wouldn't be able to enjoy. Not as long as Jean was her mother. And especially not as long as Felix was laid off from his job and without disposable income. Penelope had thought it impossible to obtain. Yet she had pined for it anyway. She'd longed for her own ten-speed each time she saw neighborhood kids riding them around. They had looked so cool. So fast. And a bike had been a sure way to spend more time away from home and away from Jean.

When Felix had told his daughter about the gift, he'd taken her to the department store to pick it out. He'd let her ride it around the aisles, trying it out. Then he'd put it on layaway so that he could make payments over time. If all went according to plan, he'd pay the last of the balance just before Penelope's birthday and he'd bring the bike home to her. The only catch: Felix told Penelope that she mustn't tell her mother about the bike. Not a word. He had stressed the fact that Jean wouldn't like it, and that she'd make him cancel the layaway if she knew. To get the bike, Penelope and her dad would need to keep it a secret.

"It's just between us," Felix had said. "You can't tell your mother. Okay?"

Young Penelope had nodded, not knowing better. She had been a kid. She had just wanted a bike like the others.

It hadn't been unreasonable. It wasn't like she had asked for a pony. Or a trip around the world. But it had been a large enough purchase that she'd had to hide it from her own mother.

"What will Mom say when you bring it home on my birthday?" Penelope had asked.

"Once it's home and she sees you riding it, she'll have to go along," Felix had said. "She isn't so cruel as to deny her child something when it's already in her hands."

Penelope had nodded, then said goodbye to her blue bike as the layaway attendant wheeled it into the back and gave Felix a claim ticket with an identifying number.

"Will it wait right there for me?" Penelope had asked, wishing she could have taken it home right away.

"Yes, babydoll," Felix had said. "It will wait right here until I get enough money to pay it off. Then I'll bring it home for your birthday. Before you know it, you'll be riding it around the neighborhood with the other kids." He knelt down in front of his daughter and gave her a tight hug. "When you're grown up, I want you to look back and remember that being a kid was fun. You deserve that. And even though times have been tough lately, I promise to always do my best for you. You're my girl, Penny."

Felix had gotten Penelope a cherry slushy and a warm, salted pretzel at the snack counter on their way out of the store. All along the ride home in Felix's little white car with red leather interior, Penelope had contemplated the need to hide news of her bike from her mother. As she had sipped her slushy through the tall straw nervously, she gulped air along with it. It was that day that she had begun holding her breath when she knew she'd have to lie. She was too young and inexperienced to navigate the subtleties of her parents' marriage, or the intricacies of her mom's mental illness. All she knew was that she couldn't tell everyone everything anymore. Not if she wanted anything fun for herself. It seemed like Jean only wanted Penelope to suffer along with her. Felix hadn't wanted that for his daughter, but the only alternative he had offered had been to hide the good things from Jean. He had said outright that it had been necessary. It had been a lot for young Penelope to handle.

When her birthday had rolled around, she had, in fact, received the shiny new ten-speed as Felix had promised. Jean had been angry, but when was she not? Her face had turned boiling red when she'd seen Felix unloading the bike from the back of his car. Penelope had done her best to ignore Jean's reaction, though it was difficult. She had jumped on the bike, and with her dad's permission, she had ridden it quickly out of the driveway and away from Jean. Felix had given his daughter her first real taste of freedom and autonomy. It had been a mixed blessing.

Through the experience, Penelope had learned several important things. She hadn't realized it at the time, but her subconscious mind had been soaking the lessons up like a sponge, cataloging them for future reference.

She had learned that she could trust her father to keep his word. Even during difficult times, he had told her she could count on him. And she had. She had also learned that to have nice things that she wanted, she had to hide them from her mother. But she had taken that even further. Deep down, Penelope felt like she didn't deserve nice things. Her nine-year-old mind wasn't sophisticated enough to understand Jean's self-esteem issues and how they had been thrust upon her daughter against her will. A part of Penelope still felt that way, even now. Only the contradicting belief also existed within her. Felix had shown Penelope that she did deserve nice things. It was a jumbled mess.

When it had come time to dispose of the money envelope, Penelope had considered turning to Felix. He had sided with her before, and it had been his idea to keep things from Jean. But Felix had been out of town, working again at a new job. And besides, Penelope had wanted her independence. She had wanted to handle things on her own. True freedom could only come from self-reliance.

Feeling clever, Penelope had hidden the envelope in the Sunnyday Sales Club folder, then taken it to school the next day where she had thrown it away in the big metal trash can in her classroom. Another hurdle had been leaped. Another step in her plan was complete.

She had kept the cash in the Sales Club folder, too. At first, she hadn't been sure exactly what to do with it, but on the fly, she had figured it out.

Sitting bored in social studies one day when she had finished her assigned work, Penelope had raised her hand and asked her teacher if it was okay to enter her sales records on the lined ledger that had been provided with the folder. Each class had been offered rewards and prizes for high sales numbers, so Penelope's teacher had been happy to allow it. Using her best penmanship, Penelope had carefully matched up gift items with addresses in her neighborhood, recalled from memory which had been learned while riding around on her bike. At her desk that day, Penelope listed fake order after fake order until the total came up to eighty-six dollars and twenty-five cents. It had taken all of her math skills to tally it properly.

When finished, Penelope had marched up to her teacher's desk and presented the cash, explaining that one of her neighbors had said to keep the extra seventy-five cents in change. Her teacher had smiled, commending Penelope for such high sales, and telling her to thank her parents for their support. Little did the teacher know, Penelope hadn't even mentioned the Sunnyday Sales Club to her parents. She'd see to that later.

It would be just like it had been with the ten-speed bike, Penelope had hoped. Once Jean saw the tent in Penelope's hands, she'd be angry, but she'd let her keep it. Felix would be proud of his daughter's deceit, since it was for good reason.

Penelope had thought it was the only way to get what she wanted. She couldn't just ask. But little had young Penelope known, things hadn't been destined to work out exactly as she had planned.

"It's Marshall! They have him!" Penelope exclaimed as she clicked the play button on the online newscast.

Penelope, Brian, and Hana sat stunned as they watched footage of Marshall being handcuffed and put into the back of a police car. Luke and Neil were there, walking confidently to their own vehicle as a uniformed officer drove Marshall away.

"That's not good," Brian mumbled.

"I can't believe it," Penelope continued. "We talked to those detectives yesterday. They told us they didn't think we were involved with Audrey's disappearance."

"Pen," Hana said. "They said a man's remains were found. This is about the blonde man. Maybe they found Marshall's DNA on his body. A strand of hair could have easily attached itself during the struggle."

Penelope's heart sank.

"Let's listen," Brian urged.

A polished female reporter named Sharonda Vinson

stood outside the Rosemary Run Police Department as she read from notes in her hand. She explained that an unidentified man's body had been found in the bay, and that, at this time, Marshall was the only suspect in his murder. She used the word murder and said she expected Marshall to be charged. Police suspected foul play.

Penelope cringed. It physically pained her to listen. Sharonda seemed smart and trustworthy. And she wasn't sensationalizing the story. She stuck to the facts, telling viewers she'd have more by the evening newscast. Once she had said her piece, she cut to an interview with Mayor John Hughes. He stood on the steps of the Rosemary Run court house and said he trusted the town's investigators to ensure justice would be done.

"We have to go to him," Penelope said, standing.

"Um, no we don't," Brian said. "Marshall is a big boy. A little stay in jail isn't going to hurt him. He's seen plenty worse."

"But…"

"Look, this seems bad," Brian continued. "But it might be a good thing. At least, we know Marshall is safer there. It would be hard for the woman you saw following you or anyone else to get to him when he's in police custody."

"That's true, Pen," Hana added. "You know it is."

"Then what?" Penelope asked.

"Then we stick to our plan," Brian confirmed. "This is one piece of information. While it's upsetting to you, I know, it's not the only piece of information we need. We have to figure out what's going on here. There's a larger picture."

"But Marshall is innocent," Penelope added. "I'm the one who choked that man out. And we were acting in self-defense. The guy was trying to kill us!"

"She's right," Hana said. "I was there for the whole thing."

"Reggie's surveillance footage will prove it," Penelope explained. "Maybe we should contact him. He's probably mad at Marshall right now for leaving him, but they love each other. Reggie wouldn't want to see Marshall jailed for a crime he didn't commit."

"Reggie? Is that the guy Marshall was married to?" Brian asked.

Penelope nodded.

"What do you think about contacting him?" Hana asked Brian.

Brian took a deep breath, then glanced out to check on Madeline. "I wouldn't advise it. Not yet. We don't know who is on our side and who isn't."

"True," Hana replied. "Marshall said something last night about Reggie not being on our side. Your phrasing reminded me of that. I think he was going to tell us more, but we sort of ran out of time. There was drama with Cheryl…"

Brian looked interested and lowered his brow. "Tell me more about that. What kind of drama?"

Hana looked to Penelope to explain.

"It wasn't a big deal," Penelope said, shrugging.

"It sounds like it might be relevant here," Brian urged. "We can't leave anything out. The first rule of investigating is to assume that every single piece of information is important. Please tell me everything."

"Okay," Penelope said, sitting back down in her chair and clasping her knees.

"It's okay, Pen," Hana said. "I know how you feel about Cheryl, but go ahead, tell Brian. He won't think any less of her. He'll respect the friendship."

Hana knew of Penelope's concern because she shared the same.

Penelope thought it was strange that just two days prior, she and Hana had been at odds. Now, they were growing closer by the minute as a result of the stress they were under. All things considered, Penelope was grateful. Hana was proving herself a good and loyal friend. She had shared what she'd seen at the party with Audrey, and she was being honest and forthcoming. It was time for Penelope to do the same.

"Okay, okay," Penelope began again. "Cheryl had an outburst last night and yelled about not trusting Marshall. He wanted her to say what she'd seen at the party so we were all on the same page, and she avoided the question. She was nervous. And volatile. I'd never seen her so jumpy, and we've known each other since grade school. But that isn't all."

"Huh," Brian said. He leaned back in his chair, settling in for what seemed like it would be a long story.

"Is there more?" Hana asked, confused.

"There is," Penelope confirmed. "Hana, I tried to tell you and Meg at the dock the morning after the party. But you didn't want to listen… and it just didn't happen."

"We were all in shock and trying to figure out what was happening that morning," Hana replied. "But you're right. I didn't listen to you. I knew you were trying to be serious, and I deflected. I wanted to avoid it." Brian eyed her. "I'm sorry."

Penelope sighed. "Thanks, Hana. I appreciate that."

"So, what is it?" Brian asked. "Time is of the essence here."

Hana nodded. "Yeah, Pen. What is it?"

Penelope steeled herself, gripping the arms of her chair. Saying what she knew would be hard for her. Really hard. It went against every coping mechanism she had learned and used in her life.

"It's tough," Penelope said. "It's… about Cheryl."

"Go on," Brian prompted.

"At the party. With Audrey… I saw…"

Her palms sweat. She felt dizzy. This was new. Penelope was used to her body reacting when she told a lie. She wasn't accustomed to its reaction when she told a hard truth. It felt scary, but also good. She liked being honest.

"Go ahead, Pen," Hana said. "It's okay. You're among friends."

"Fine," Penelope said, shaking her head as if she could shake the nervousness out. "At the party, Hana, remember the guys you saw who drugged Audrey and led her into the pool?"

"Of course I do."

"And then the guy Cheryl told us about seeing hitting on Audrey? The one she said looked like Bradley Cooper?"

"Yeah. So?"

"Earlier in the evening, I saw Cheryl talking with all three of them. And I saw her slip a small vial of something to one of them."

"Oh!" Hana exclaimed. "Like the vial I saw the one guy use to put something in Audrey's drink?"

"I think so," Penelope said. "I think Cheryl was in on it. Like, I think she was working with them."

"Huh," Brian said again, reaching for a pad of paper in the drawer in front of him. He grabbed a pen and took notes.

"Wow," Hana said. "Our Cheryl? *Your* Cheryl? Did you confront her?"

"Yes, our Cheryl. And, no. I didn't confront her. She came to my condo yesterday saying she had to tell me something. I was going to talk to her about what I saw, but as soon as she heard about me and Marshall being together, she shut it down. Wouldn't tell me a thing. So, I let it go, too. I figured there would be time. I was planning to talk to Marshall about it. And now..."

Hana shook her head.

"I just hate it, though," Penelope continued. "Cheryl was still happy for me... during our conversation yesterday. She was still being my friend. But she seemed conflicted. We've been friends for so long. I can't imagine losing her. That's why I've waited to say anything. I've been trying to make sense of it in my mind. And then, with the way she blew up at Marshall last night... It seemed like she wanted to throw him off her trail. You know?"

"I can see that," Hana said. "Just, wow."

Brian scribbled furiously, making charts and circles with arrows in between.

"What are you thinking?" Penelope asked him.

"I don't know yet," he replied. "But let's look at the loyalties here. Marshall was connected to Reggie, but now says Reggie isn't on your side. Again, I trust Marshall, so I'm automatically on his. When you spend time in country with someone like I did with Marshall, you learn their character. You *have* to rely on the people by your side in that kind of hostile situation. And Marshall proved himself again and again. My money's on Marshall being a good guy. So, if we move from there, we have to assume that Reggie is not a good guy. At least, not in this particular situation."

"Right," Hana agreed.

"Let's line up the bad actors in one column: Reggie, Cheryl…"

Penelope winced as Brian said her oldest friend's name. Even though it was true, it still hurt. It reminded her a lot of when Zach said something negative about their mother. He was quicker to point out Jean's shortcomings and the effect her behavior had on her children.

Brian continued. "Three guys at the party… Let's identify them. There's the one that looks like Bradley Cooper."

"Yeah, Cheryl called him Cooper Clone," Penelope added. "And Hana said she'd do Bradley Cooper."

"Pen!" Hana exclaimed. "What is wrong with you? Because I honestly wonder sometimes."

Brian chuckled. "Okay, Cooper Clone. What do we

call the others? There's the guy that slipped something into Audrey's drink, right?"

"Yeah," Penelope said. "Drink guy."

"And the guy who led her into the pool. Pool guy?"

"That works. So, we add them to the bad actor list along with the blonde man in the bay, and the blonde woman on the motorcycle. Yes?"

"Yes," Penelope and Hana said.

Brian continued to scribble. "And good actors are Marshall, the two of you… Who else? Meg?"

Penelope and Hana looked at each other. Neither wanted to implicate their friend without evidence. They didn't know what to think about Meg.

"It's hard to say for sure," Penelope explained. "She seemed to be telling the truth last night. And Marshall seemed to believe her."

"Good," Brian confirmed. "Good column for now. What did she say?"

Hana jumped in, pulling her knees to her chest. Her pose reminded Penelope of the other morning on the dock and just how far they'd come since then.

"That she had been entertaining a doctor from San Francisco in the library all night. She said they were listening to a jazz quartet and didn't leave the room until first responders were on the scene."

"Wait," Brian said. "Go back. I thought you said Audrey had disappeared."

"Yeah, that's right," Penelope confirmed. "Then what were first responders doing there?"

"That's a good question," Hana replied. "I don't know. I didn't call them. Did you, Pen?"

"No."

"Huh," Brian replied.

His mannerisms were similar to Marshall's. Penelope noted that it must be a Marine thing.

"Okay," he continued. "We'll put a pin in that. We don't necessarily need to know what everyone at the party was doing, as long as we figure out what is relevant to us. And to proving Marshall's innocence. We'll go back to that if need be. Tell me more about the characters closely involved. Anybody we've missed?"

Penelope ran a hand through her hair as she thought. Her body was relaxing more now that she had spilled the beans on Cheryl.

"There's the doorman at my building," Hana blurted, remembering.

"Oh? What's his name?" Brian asked.

"Zeke Finley. The blonde woman asked him about me. He's the one that tipped me off to the fact that she was following me."

"And how much do you know about him?" Brian asked.

"Not much," Hana explained. "He's been my doorman for a year and a half or so, but all we do is make small talk."

"Okay, then," Brian continued. "We can't really put him in any column. We'll make a new one for unknown." He scribbled more, his charts looking almost unintelligible at this point. "Anyone else? Anyone at all."

"Meg named the prospective client from San Francisco that she was courting: Dr. Mitch Bowker," Hana added. "Unknown."

"And there's my brother," Penelope added. "He isn't involved yet, but once he realizes I'm missing, he's likely to get involved. Zach Cline. Add him to the good column. No doubt."

"Does he live in Rosemary Run?" Brian asked.

"Yes."

"Good," Brian said again. "I'll compile a fact sheet for each person. I'll share the doc with the two of you and I want you to make a bullet point list, adding every minuscule piece of information you can think of related to their involvement here. Make note of what they look like, who they hang out with, what their motivations might be, and anything else you can think of. I mean it. Everything. Then we'll start digging."

"Okay," Penelope agreed.

She thought about Marshall and how he must be feeling, trapped behind bars. He was probably worried about her. He wouldn't know for sure that she had made it to Brian's. She thought maybe she should try to get a message to him.

"Brian?" Penelope asked. Hana had leaned her head on Brian's shoulder while she waited for him to create the document.

"Yeah?"

"Marshall mentioned that you might have burner phones for us?"

"I do, but we have to be careful. Who do you want to call?"

Penelope sighed. "I want to let Marshall know we're okay. He's probably worried sick."

Brian shook his head. "Penelope, I know you just met

me last night, but please, trust me on this. The advantage we have right now is secrecy. No one knows where the two of you are except Marshall, and I guarantee you he won't tell anybody. We only have one bunker. We can't risk leading anyone here."

21

For two long days, Penelope and Hana stayed at Brian's house with him and Madeline. No one left. And no one arrived. The four of them enjoyed each other's company, none more so than Brian and Hana. They cooked delicious food, watched movies, and even sang along with Brian accompanying on acoustic guitar. It was good. But it wasn't enough for Penelope.

As for solving the mysteries and luring the bad guys so they wouldn't be a threat to Hana and Penelope's safety, progress was slow. Brian, Penelope, and Hana worked together on internet research, and Brian made inquiries with some of his contacts in the intelligence community. In fact, it turned out that Brian had worked in military intelligence. He told the ladies stories from his time in the service and entertained them with near misses that would have changed the world had the public known what had happened. Penelope wondered if Marshall had worked in intelligence, too. She inquired with Brian, but he insisted that Marshall would need to answer that question himself.

The three adults put their heads together, and as a result, they compiled a ton of information about everyone on their lists. They scoured news reports and internet chatter, including on the dark web. It was solid work. Brian reiterated that these things took time. He reminded them they were safe, and that was the primary goal.

But Penelope was growing restless. Marshall was still in jail, and she was desperate to do something to help him. She had found the courage to jump on the blonde man's back the day he attacked Marshall on the dock, and she knew she could do something like it again if she had to. She regretted running away and leaving her love when the dog had attacked. She felt more and more like she should have stayed to help Marshall in any way she could. Maybe then he wouldn't be in jail. Maybe the two of them could be snuggling and cuddling together, like Brian and Hana.

When Brian said he and Madeline needed to leave the house for a while to go check on his elderly mother, Penelope hatched a plan. She would wait until Brian was gone. Then, she'd use his tech room to get a message out to Zach. She could trust Zach. She knew that much for sure. She'd initiate a phone call using Brian's landline upstairs to tell her brother what was happening, and she'd ask him to go to Marshall to let him know she was okay.

It seemed like a decent idea. She wouldn't leave the property. And she wouldn't contact Marshall directly. As far as Penelope could predict, a phone call to her brother wouldn't cause any trouble. The only snag: she needed to do all of this without Hana knowing. Penelope was sure that Hana would tell Brian if she found out. Her allegiance was to him now. Penelope didn't mind or blame her friend, but she wanted to keep this to herself.

What Penelope would do about her breathing situation, she wasn't entirely sure.

"We won't be gone long," Brian said as he and Madeline packed up a bag of toys and snacks. They were all upstairs in the house. The sun was shining brightly outside. "Everything you need is down in the bunker. I recommend you stay down there, but I understand if you need a little daylight. Just stay indoors."

He showed them a hidden key and demonstrated the fastest way to lock down the bunker.

"Don't worry about us," Hana said. "You two go. We'll be here when you get back." She kissed him on the lips. Madeline didn't seem to mind her father's new relationship. She liked Hana, and she smiled when they kissed.

"You sure you'll be okay?" he asked, looking at Hana but eyeing Penelope to the side.

Penelope stayed quiet. She didn't want to be backed into a corner and forced to lie. She knew that wouldn't go well. She focused on saying what was true.

"We're grown women," she said, teasing. "And we've each lived alone for most of our adult lives. We'll be fine. Go!"

Brian kissed Hana again before stepping outside with Madeline and locking the door behind him. He promised to return by sundown, in plenty of time to watch an evening movie together and get Madeline tucked into bed.

As his truck pulled out of the driveway, Hana turned

to Penelope and squealed. "OMG!" she said. "Can you believe this, Pen? He is dreamy!"

"You sound like a schoolgirl with a crush," Penelope replied, though she knew their relationship was much more than that.

"Don't do that," Hana said.

"Do what?"

"Deflect. Minimize. Be jealous."

Penelope sighed as she plopped down on Brian's sofa. "You're right. I know. I'm just kidding, but I shouldn't kid. I see what the two of you have. It looks a lot like love at first sight."

"I know!" Hana said, her voice returning to its original happy tone. "It's like we… like we…"

"Like you belong together."

"Exactly!" Hana confirmed. "I never would have thought Brian was my type, but oh, is he ever. And in bed…" She rolled her eyes back in her head and parted her lips.

"I feel the same about Marshall. At least you didn't push him away and send him into the arms of someone else… like I did. That wasn't my finest hour," Penelope explained.

Hana sat down on the sofa next to her friend. "I get it. But you're together now. Everything worked out okay in the end."

"Is that what you'd call this? Marshall is in jail and I'm stuck here, like a prisoner."

"Pen," Hana said with a sigh. "Don't be so dramatic. I'm supposed to be the drama queen, remember? Don't go stealing my role. Our entire friendship might crumble."

They laughed.

"You miss him, don't you?" Hana asked softly.

"I really do. I can hardly stand it."

They stared at each other, then out the front window. Neither of them had an answer as to what they should do. At least, not one that Penelope wanted to share with Hana. She hoped Hana would hurry up and get out of her hair somehow so that she could get in touch with Zach.

"It reminds me of my mom," Penelope said, seemingly out of the blue and surprising Hana.

"Oh, really? How so?"

"She used to complain all the time about being a prisoner in her own home. I'm not sure, but I think that was one of the main things she was angry about. I think she resented me and Zach for needing taken care of. As if we were the reason she was stuck at home."

"That doesn't even make logical sense," Hana replied. "Your dad wasn't abusive or anything, was he?"

"No," Penelope answered. "Not that I know of. Certainly not to me. My parents yelled and screamed at each other quite a bit. At least, once Zach was born, and we moved to Rosemary Run. My mom was unhappy here. She missed her family and friends in Washington State, where we had lived previously. She had grown up there. Dad had, too. Then they moved here for Dad's job. Mom hated it."

"Still," Hana said, "she could have gotten a job to get out of the house, right? She could have made some friends. It isn't fair to pin that on you. Or your Dad. Hell!"

"I know. I don't think he knew what to do with her.

And I don't think she was normal. I mean, I think she had something wrong with her. Maybe more than one thing."

"That sucks," Hana said, chewing on a fingernail. She'd been letting them be since they'd arrived at Brian's, but Penelope's childhood was apparently stressing her out.

"It sure does."

"How long ago did she die? Twelve years ago now?"

Penelope took a deep breath before answering. It was still painful. "She's been gone twelve years. Almost thirteen. And Dad's been gone eleven."

Hana shook her head. "I'm no expert," she said. "But it doesn't seem normal for you to be this upset this many years later. I think you have trauma that needs released. Especially if you want to have a good relationship with Marshall. You know?"

"You're probably right," Penelope said.

"I know I am," Hana replied. "I've been your friend long enough to watch you play it safe and wait on the sidelines of life. You can't keep doing that if you want true happiness. You have to go out there and get it."

Tears fell from Penelope's eyes as she listened. She knew Hana was exactly right. She'd been thinking about the same thing herself lately. Her childhood trauma was a secret she'd buried for far too long. She didn't usually talk about it. She tried not to even think about it. But it affected her. It was a jumble of burdens that felt heavy and sticky, like quicksand or tar. Penelope knew that she could either hide her hurts and remain a prisoner of her own accord, or she could face them and set herself free. Being with Marshall would necessitate setting herself free.

Especially if she wanted children. And she did want children.

"I want to go get my happiness," Penelope confirmed, thinking about her plan to reach Zach. "I want to be brave, to both get what I want and stop letting the past hold me back. I'm just not sure exactly how to do that."

Hana turned to face her friend and put one hand on her shoulder.

"What?" Penelope asked. "Are you going to break it down into steps for me?"

"Maybe I should," Hana replied. "Especially with Cheryl on the outs. I might have to step up and take over some of her duties."

Penelope slumped down at mention of Cheryl's name. That was another sore spot. And it somehow felt tangled up with the feelings from her childhood. She furrowed her brow, tears continuing to roll down her cheeks. "I… It's a tangled mess, Hana. I don't know what to say. As strange as you are, you seem to have a normal family. Normal parents. Normal siblings. The same goes for Cheryl and Meg. You all have perspective that I don't seem to. You know how to behave in ways that I don't. But at the same time, the way Cheryl acted the other day reminded me so much of my mom. It's hard to make sense out of it."

Hana patted Penelope's shoulder and looked at her sympathetically. "Hey, it's okay. There are therapists that help with this sort of thing. And books. Help is out there. You're smart. You can sort it out."

"Yeah," Penelope said, nodding.

They were quiet for a minute as they contemplated their situation.

"It's just bizarre, though," Penelope said. "The way things are happening. The danger. The police investigation. Why now?"

"I'd like to know the answer to that, too," Hana said with a chuckle, taking her hand back. "But I won't look the gift horse in the mouth. I'm a lucky lady to have found Brian like this. I'm not sure how else we would have met."

"Yeah."

"Hey," Hana said, trying to sound encouraging. "You said the situation with the party and Audrey's disappearance helped you decide to tell Marshall how you felt, right? So it brought you two together the same as it did for me and Brian."

"You're right again," Penelope said. "I guess I shouldn't be so negative… My mom used to say that. That no one likes a negative nelly. She used to berate me, Hana. It was bad."

"Aw."

"I look at Madeline, and I wonder how a mother could be so cruel to an innocent child like she was to me. I was only a few years older than Madeline when my mom really started laying into me. I don't care how frustrated they are. A grown adult shouldn't take their anger out on a child. Especially not their own. What did I ever do to deserve that?"

"Nothing, Pen. Absolutely nothing."

"I'm a good person," Penelope said. "Truly, I am."

Hana sighed. "I know."

Suddenly, there was a knock at the front door. The sound rattled the screen and echoed through the little house. Penelope glanced in that direction, but couldn't see who was there.

"What should we do?" Hana asked. "We'd have to go all the way downstairs to see the camera feed."

"That seems like a flaw in Brian's system."

"Not really. He has the feed on his smartphone, too. He probably knows who's here. We could call him."

"Nah," Penelope said. "That's silly. We're right here. Let's look out the window first to see what we can, then we'll open the door."

"Pen! It's dangerous."

"Yeah, well, I'm getting a little tired of being cooped up, anyway. Aren't you?"

Hana didn't answer. She followed Penelope to the window. They looked out, but didn't see anyone.

"Nothing," Penelope whispered.

Another knock came. Louder this time. And a young woman's voice. "Is anyone there?"

The voice was familiar to them both. Hana cocked her head to one side, trying to place it. It took her a minute, but finally, Hana remembered. She smiled with recognition and went to the door. "No way," she breathed.

"Who?" Penelope asked.

Hana opened the door, confirming her recollection. Standing in front of them was the person they least expected to see.

"Audrey! What are you doing here?"

22

"We thought you were dead!" Hana said. "How… ? What… ?"

"Nice to see you again, too," Audrey replied. "Are you going to let me in?"

Hana and Penelope looked at each other. Penelope nodded. "Yes. Come in."

They led Audrey to the sofa and fastened the deadbolts behind her. Penelope took a seat in Brian's chair. Hana sat down beside Audrey.

"Did you come alone?" Penelope asked.

Hana shot her a look that said she was being rude. But Penelope wanted to be careful. There was a lot they didn't understand.

"Yep, just me," Audrey said.

Her demeanor was different than it had been at the party. She seemed more relaxed. Also, more mature. She no longer seemed like a girl who might have been underage. Maybe it had been an act.

"Did you arrive on foot?" Penelope inquired,

imagining what Brian or Marshall would ask and then following that lead.

"I did. Same as you."

"Wait," Hana said, raising a hand in the air. "*What?* How do you know how we got here?"

"Because Marshall sent me."

She said it matter-of-factly. Like it wasn't a big deal. Penelope nearly fell out of her chair.

"Marshall who?"

"Marshall Erving. Are we really going to play that game?"

"I…" Penelope was flabbergasted.

She wondered if Audrey was dangerous. Might she have been the one with the attack dog? And could she have been watching them the day Penelope and Hana had arrived at Brian's? None of it made sense.

Hana took a breath, then tried her turn. "Audrey…"

"Please, call me Marta. That's my real name."

"What?" Hana's brows lowered, and she absentmindedly put a finger in her mouth and chewed on the nail.

"I'm Marta Pavlo. Go on."

This was a lot for Penelope and Hana to take in.

"Okay, Marta," Hana said hesitantly. "I don't mean to intrude, but I saw that man drug you at Reggie's party. And then I saw the other one lead you into the pool while you were out of it. And the EMTs… they pulled you out of the pool. I thought…"

"It was all a cover," Marta said. "I'm a federal agent. I'm fine. Fit as a fiddle."

"Wait!" Hana blurted. "This is silly. It can't be real. Come on, now. Tell us the truth."

Penelope shook her head, trying to process. She quickly went through the motions in her mind. If Audrey… err, Marta… was a federal agent, then Marshall must be, too? Right? They must have been working undercover to take down the guys Reggie had gotten himself involved with. Maybe that was why Marshall had married Reggie. Maybe it had all been an act. And maybe Brian worked with them. Because… Well, what did he actually do for work, anyway? Was he just a stay-at-home dad who happened to have a high-tech underground bunker? There had to be more to that story. Her thoughts swirled as she attempted to make sense of it.

"It's real. Keep up," Marta said with a laugh.

"So, do you have a badge of something?" Hana asked.

"That would defeat the purpose of working undercover, don't you think?"

Hana nodded. "Okay, I guess I can see that. But how do we know you're telling the truth?"

Marta tapped her fingers on her knee as she thought about it. "I guess you can't. Until this is all over, anyway. Then the local police will confirm my cover story."

"The Rosemary Run police?" Penelope asked.

"Those are the ones."

"Detectives Luke Hemming and Neil Fredericks?"

"Yep," Marta said, glibly.

She seemed so unconcerned.

Penelope stood and motioned for Hana to join her in the kitchen. "Hana, a word?"

Hana looked at Marta.

"Go ahead," Marta said, waving a hand. "Talk amongst yourselves. We've got nothing but time. I'm hanging out with you two until this thing blows up and then blows over."

Hana excused herself and she and Penelope scurried to the kitchen where they could have a more private conversation while still keeping an eye on Marta.

"Do you believe what she's saying is true?" Penelope whispered in her friend's ear. "Because it frightens me that we have no way to check."

"I know," Hana agreed. "Brian won't be back for hours. We don't have phones of our own and aren't supposed to use the ones at the house."

"Even if the undercover agent thing is true, we don't know if she's on our side. We didn't even add her to the list of good and bad actors. It seems like an obvious oversight now. But it could be some kind of trap," Penelope said. "And we just let her in. Like a Trojan Horse."

"Right," Hana confirmed. "She says her last name is Pavlo, yeah?"

Penelope nodded.

"Doesn't that sound Eastern European to you? Or Russian?"

"I thought so, too. And the blonde man from the dock and his look-alike female cohort who was following me… if I didn't know better, I'd say they were Russian."

"If I had to guess," Hana said, "I'd agree."

"Something is going on here," Penelope proclaimed. "Something serious."

They stood silently, gazing at Marta. She smiled back at them, then waved. It was odd how relaxed she seemed.

"Pen," Hana began again. "If Marshall sent her… Do you think he's some kind of agent, too? And Brian?"

"Seems that way," Penelope confirmed. Neither wanted to think about it, let alone say it. But Penelope gave voice to her doubts. "Do you think they're using us? That our love stories aren't real?"

Hana closed her eyes and leaned back against the counter. "God, I hope not. But I don't know who to trust."

"Me," Penelope confirmed. "You can trust me."

The friends hugged quickly, but then broke it up, not wanting to show Marta weakness in case they had to be tough with her later on.

"Look," Hana said. "What I feel from Brian is real. We all know his love for Madeline is real. And he trusts Marshall. *You* trust Marshall. Let's lean into that. Besides, we don't have much choice."

Penelope nodded, and they started toward the living room. "Wait," she said, grabbing Hana's arm. "One more thing before we go back in there."

"Yeah?"

Just the thought of it made Penelope take big gulps of air. "Damn," she said, mostly to herself.

"You can tell me," Hana assured.

"It's not a big deal, really," Penelope began. "It's just… I had planned to get a message out to Zach this afternoon. I wasn't going to tell you."

"Whatever," Hana said, surprising Penelope. "I figured. I wasn't going to let you out of my sight."

They laughed together. Marta eyed them from the living room, tipping her head.

"So all that heart to heart talk was a ruse to keep me busy?"

"Hey, now," Hana said. "You're the one who launched into your origin story."

"My origin story?" Penelope asked with a chuckle. "What am I? A superhero?"

"Maybe."

Hana winked at her friend. "Come on. If Marta was really sent by Marshall, that means he's okay. And it means that he probably knows you're okay. Maybe all we really need to do is let the professionals work without getting in their way."

"You're right. Maybe that's why Marshall sent us here. Our seclusion serves the dual purpose of keeping us safe and out of their way."

"Brian and Marshall have probably been in touch," Hana said. "Especially if Luke and Neil are in on this. In fact, Marshall's arrest is probably part of the cover."

They agreed with each other. It felt good to be on the same page. Feeling determined, but curious, they returned to the living room. They sat down, piecing things together in their minds as they looked at Marta.

"Okay," Penelope said. "We're beginning to get it. But please humor us awhile longer. When did you last have contact with Marshall?"

Marta smiled. "This morning."

Something about the way she said it sent a wave of jealousy coursing through Penelope. Marshall was her man. And she didn't want a young, beautiful secret agent smiling about him like that.

"Easy," Hana said, sensing Penelope's reaction.

Penelope took a breath. "Did you talk with him in person?"

"Yep," Marta replied. "We had breakfast at the station."

"The police station?"

"Yep."

Penelope wanted to ask a lot more. But she didn't want to seem jealous. She'd never felt so strongly about a man. This was new to her. It suddenly felt like no one could possibly understand how much she needed him.

"Relax," Marta said, finally. "He told me about the two of you. He's yours, Penelope. No funny business from me. Marshall and I are colleagues. Nothing more."

Penelope exhaled hard, sputtering as if she had been telling a lie. Only she hadn't. It was her body's reaction to caring so much.

Hana smiled on behalf of her friend. "Thank you for saying that, Marta."

"So, Marshall's a federal agent?" Penelope asked.

"He is," Marta replied. "He said you might ask about that. And he said to tell you the truth. He was going to do that as soon as this case wraps up."

"His marriage… ? To Reggie?"

"Part of deep cover," Marta replied.

Penelope practically went limp, the relief on her face plain to see. "And… ?"

"His love for you is real," the young woman confirmed.

Hana stood and squealed, running over to hug her friend. "I told you! See? You knew it. We all knew it."

Penelope smiled. Despite the drama going on around her and the shock at hearing confirmation of Marshall's top-secret occupation, she felt happy and content. She knew that a life with a federal agent might be difficult, and that it might involve danger. But as long as she and Marshall had each other, they could get through anything.

Now, if she could just see him again so they could talk about all of this. Penelope missed Marshall terribly.

By the time Brian's red and white truck pulled into the driveway, Marta, Penelope, and Hana had gotten comfortable with each other. Marta had explained much more about Reggie's operation and how he had inadvertently gotten tangled up with a human trafficking ring based in Russia. She had told the ladies how the lesser-evil escort service had been a cover for what they were really interested in, and that had been trafficking young girls and selling them to the highest bidders.

Marta had described Reggie as a decent guy who had gotten mixed up with the wrong crowd. She had said he'd been lured in by the taste of money and had been manipulated into participating in criminal activity that ran contrary to what he really believed in and wanted. Once in, he hadn't known how to get himself out. The Russians had kept close tabs on his every move and had threatened his life if he didn't cooperate.

That's where Marshall had come into the picture. On assignment and with the support of local police, he had befriended Reggie under cover, going as far as to fake a relationship with him to gain access to the Russian trafficking ring. Marta had been called in from D.C. to assist. It had all been set to go down the night of the party. Marshall and Marta had been close to obtaining the evidence they needed to nab the Russians. A team of additional federal agents had been in place and ready to assist local authorities. But there had been unexpected interference from a local woman. It had been enough for them to keep the cover in place a while longer while they continued to investigate her involvement.

Marta had said it was all done now, and that authorities would announce the real arrests shortly. Marshall would be free to go about his life unencumbered. At least, until he received his next assignment.

Brian's key clanked against the lock as the screen door creaked. "I'm home!" he called out, stepping inside with a grin on his face. Madeline made her way from behind his legs and skipped into the living room.

"Hi, Marta!" Madeline said.

Marta picked the girl up and spun her around, kissing her cheeks.

"You two know each other?" Penelope asked, making the connections.

"We do," Marta replied. "Madeline and I are coloring buddies. We take turns with coloring books when I get breaks from work downstairs."

"Ah, I see," Penelope replied. "So, the bunker isn't just for Brian's overzealous doomsday prepping?"

"Nope," Marta confirmed.

"Who would have thought?" Penelope mused. "A base

of operations like that, right here in little old Rosemary Run…"

Hana rushed to Brian, leaping into his arms and wrapping herself tightly around him. They kissed passionately, oblivious to anyone else in the room. Penelope, Marta, and Madeline all smiled. Hana and Brian made a good couple. An excellent couple, in fact.

"Penelope," Brian said. "I brought someone with me who wants to see you."

Brian reached back to open the door once more, and in stepped Marshall. His face was beaming with the most genuine happy smile Penelope had ever seen. "There's my girl," he said as he winked at her and opened his arms wide.

"Marshall!" Penelope exclaimed. She ran to him, practically knocking the coffee table over as she went. She jumped all the way up onto him, latching on with her legs around his waist and her arms around his neck. "My hero! I've missed you so much."

"Not as much as I've missed you," he said softly, kissing both of her cheeks and then her lips, deeply. Her body warmed to his touch.

"Oh, Marshall," Penelope said as he held her. "I had no idea before. Marta explained everything. It's all going to be okay."

"So, you're not mad at me for sticking you here and letting you think I was in jail?"

"Maybe a little," Penelope teased. "But it's all good. You were working undercover. I get it. I'm proud of you."

"I was deep undercover," Marshall explained. "For more than two years. Once the blonde guy, Vlad, died in the bay, we knew others would come looking. His death wasn't according to plan, but once it happened, we had to be sure our cover wasn't blown until we caught all the criminals involved in this thing."

"And that's all done now?" Penelope asked. "Can we go home to my condo?"

Marshall and Brian glanced at each other.

"Almost," Brian said.

Hana looked quizzically at him.

Marta and Madeline were busy playing at the dining room table. They were opening cans of putty without a care in the world. Marta was hardly paying attention to the discussion happening in the next room.

"What do you mean, almost?" Hana asked.

Marshall took a deep breath. "Come, sit with me," he said to Penelope as he led her to the sofa. They sat beside each other, Marshall's arm around Penelope's shoulders and his other hand on her knee. It was a protective stance. Penelope loved it.

"You, too, Hana," Brian said. He sat down in his chair and pulled Hana onto his lap. He kissed her again. He couldn't seem to help it. She smiled brightly in return.

Marshall eyed Brian, who nodded. Neither of them wanted to be the bearer of bad news.

"Just say it," Hana said. "Whatever it is."

"It's about Cheryl," Marshall said. "Pen, Brian told me what you saw at the party… How Cheryl seemed to be involved with the trafficking ring."

Penelope began to sip air, her body anticipating a lie.

"Relax," Marshall said. "No one is upset with you for not reporting it to Luke and Neil. They understand. They got what they needed. By the time Brian filled me in on what you'd seen, the detectives already had the evidence for another source."

Penelope exhaled, softly. It hurt to hear that Cheryl was in trouble, but she was incredibly relieved that she didn't have to lie about or hide anything. She wasn't sure she could have if she'd had to.

"Was she involved?" Hana asked. "Did she participate in drugging Audrey… I mean, Marta… like Pen thought?"

"Unfortunately, yes," Marshall said. "Cheryl worked with Reggie and the Russians to drug young girls so they could be taken, then sold."

"Wow," Hana said.

"We don't think Cheryl wanted to be involved," Marshall added. "Somehow, she got roped into it. Luke suspects that one of the Russians had threatened her parents. We don't have confirmation of that yet, but it seems likely. If that's the case, she'll get a lesser sentence. But Pen, she's going to prison. There's no way around it."

Penelope shook her head, sad for her oldest friend. "And Meg?"

"Meg's in the clear, same as you two," Brian said.

It relieved Penelope and Hana to hear that. They both nodded.

Hana leaned down and nuzzled Brian's nose. "And honey, to state the obvious, you, too, are a federal agent, correct?"

"I am," he confirmed.

"Madeline? And Jessa?"

"The stories I told you about my personal life are all

true. When Jessa died, I knew I couldn't leave Madeline to travel on assignment. I tried to quit, but they wanted to keep me. We made a deal where I could stay home in Rosemary Run and man the operations center underground. I provide support to agents in the region without having to leave my house."

"Lucky bastard," Marshall said, chuckling.

"So, the part about you two serving in Iraq together?" Penelope asked.

"True. All true."

"Your elderly mother?" Hana tried.

"True. Saw her this afternoon and picked up Marshall on the way home."

Penelope shook her head again. "It's just so much to take in."

"Same," Hana agreed.

There was a moment of silence as they reflected on things. Madeline giggled from the next room as she and Marta compared coloring pages and said something about purple elephants and blue zebras. The mood felt happy. It felt light, despite the seriousness of what they'd just been through.

"Pen?" Marshall asked. "Would you like to call her?"

Penelope drew back, startled. "Cheryl?"

"Yeah."

"I can do that?"

"Brian and I can arrange it. If you want."

Tears sprang from Penelope's eyes. "Yes, please. Very much, yes."

24

When young Penelope had returned home from school the day she had sat in her classroom and carefully listed fake orders for the Sunnyday Sales Club, she had been a bundle of emotions. She had felt at the same time both confident and terrified. She'd been confident of her gumption and willingness to take action to get what she'd wanted. But she'd been terrified of what would happen to her, and even more, she'd been terrified of what her actions said about her character.

Penelope had been quiet that evening, barely saying a word at dinner. Her mind had spun as she'd tried her best to analyze the possibilities. She had wondered what she'd do with all the merchandise when it came in. She hadn't been sure she could hide it in her room. It had been too small of a space, and besides, Jean wouldn't have given her the necessary privacy. She had thought that maybe she'd tell her dad, and had hoped that Felix would help her keep the things hidden, like he'd done with the ten-speed bike.

It had been at that moment when Penelope identified the feeling she'd had. It had been about feeling bad. Simple as that. She had felt bad about herself. And not only had she felt bad about herself, she had felt like she *was* bad. The realization had stung. She was bad, and she had to hide it from others. She'd had to stuff it somewhere, hidden, just like she'd have to stuff the fake gift orders from the Sunnyday Sales Club if she wanted to get the green tent.

Jean had known how bad Penelope was. She had looked at her with disdain and had reminded her of her shortcomings nearly every day. And now, Penelope had internalized it, believing that she was bad, too.

Only a contradiction had remained within her. Deep down, she'd known she was a good person.

When the merchandise had come in, she'd told her mom that the orders had been real and that neighbors were waiting on her to deliver.

Sip. Sip. Hold.

Penelope had delivered the items on her bike, telling neighbors that they had received bonus gifts.

Sip. Sip. Sip. Hold.

She'd tried to ignore their bewildered faces as she tossed them candles, greeting cards, and picture frames as fast as she could. She'd had to get rid of the merchandise so she wouldn't get caught.

It had been one of the greatest disappointments of Penelope's young life when she got to the bottom of the bag and realized that the green tent wasn't in there. It had been set to arrive separately. What Penelope had anticipated even less was the printed statement from her savings account that had arrived at her home, notating the withdrawal of some eighty-seven dollars.

When Penelope had gotten done delivering the fake orders, she had arrived at her house to find both of her parents waiting with angry looks on their faces. Jean had raged, while Felix had told her how disappointed he was. Crushed, Penelope had told them about the green tent and how badly she had wanted it. Felix had said that Penelope should have just asked.

It had been too late for that. And besides, by that point, the tent hadn't much mattered. When it had finally arrived, her parents had sent it back. Young Penelope's beliefs about herself and how to get what she wanted out of life had been cemented. It would take decades for her to shed the emotional baggage.

25

"Cheryl?" Penelope said softly when Luke handed her friend the phone.

"Pen!" Cheryl said. "I'm so sorry. Please don't hate me."

"I couldn't."

"You should."

"I hear they threatened your family?" Penelope asked.

Cheryl began to cry. "Yes, they did. But that doesn't make what I did right. Those girls…"

"I agree," Penelope said. "You'll have to live with that."

"It will haunt me to my dying day," Cheryl said.

There was a long silence. Penelope wasn't sure what to say.

"Hey, Marshall and I are really happy together. So, something good came out of all of this. I'm not sure we would have met if it hadn't been for the escort service and his undercover assignment."

"That's good," Cheryl said. "I'm happy for you. Really. I am."

"I didn't think I deserved real happiness before," Penelope said. "I didn't have the guts to go after it. And believe it or not, you helped bring back old hurts related to my mom. I finally faced them head on and I realized that she was hurting, just like you. Both of you were in over your heads-- you with this and her with untreated mental illness. You both had your reasons for doing what you did. You didn't set out to hurt girls any more than my mom set out to hurt me and Zach. I can see that clearly now."

"Pen…"

"No, don't say anything else," Penelope urged, her voice soft but strong. "It doesn't make what you did okay, but I forgive you. Both of you."

"Oh, Pen…"

"No, wait. I forgive you for myself. So *I* can move on. But I have to let you go. Just like I have to let my mom go. I'm done. This is goodbye, Cheryl."

Penelope wiped tears from her eyes as she hung up the phone, releasing a deep breath she had been holding for the final time. She told her body sternly that she was done sipping air and holding her breath.

Instead, she'd live a life where she didn't have to feel bad about herself. She told herself she was letting those who had weighed her down go. She'd remember the good times, but she wouldn't let them hold any power over her now.

Instead, she'd live her happy life with Marshall in the little blue cottage with the big yard. They'd have the puppies and the little girl, and their little girl would be treated with nothing but love and respect.

On warm summer nights when Marshall was home and the crickets sang in the night breeze, the three of them would camp in the backyard in their big green tent. They'd do their best to live happily ever after.

THE END.

———

Get the next book in the series:

Her Worst Mistake
Rosemary Run - Book Six
www.kellyutt.com/novels/her-worst-mistake

———

BONUS CONTENT -

Rosemary Run Short Story

Get a FREE prequel short story exclusively when you sign up for Kelly's email newsletter at kellyutt.com:

Her Troubled Mind

———

Sample Kelly's newest series, The Summer Isle, with a FREE prequel short story exclusively when you sign up for her email newsletter at kellyutt.com:

The Boy on Sunset and Main

ENJOY THIS BOOK?

A NOTE FROM AUTHOR KELLY UTT

Did you enjoy this book? You can make a big difference.

Reviews are the most powerful tools in my arsenal when it comes to getting attention for my books. As much as I'd like to, I don't have the financial muscle of a New York publisher. I can't take out full page ads in the newspaper or put posters on the subway.

(Not yet, anyway.)

But I do have something much more effective than that, and it's something that those publishers would kill to get their hands on.

A committed and loyal group of readers.

Honest reviews of my books help bring them to the attention of other readers.

If you've enjoyed this book, I would be very grateful if you could spend just five minutes leaving a review (it can be as short as you like) on the book's Amazon page and on Goodreads or BookBub.

Thank you very much.

ALSO BY KELLY UTT

Have you read them all?

————

In the Rosemary Run Series

In the charming Northern California town of Rosemary Run, there's trouble brewing below the picture-perfect surface. Don't let the manicured lawns and stylish place settings fool you. Nothing is exactly as it seems. Secrets and lies threaten to upend the status quo and destroy lives when— not if— they're revealed.

SHORT STORY PREQUEL - HER TROUBLED MIND

Download it Free at Kelly's website: kellyutt.com

BOOK 1 - HER DEEPEST FEAR

BOOK 2 - HER HIDDEN PAST

BOOK 3 - HER BOLDEST LIE

BOOK 4 - HER DARKEST HOUR

BOOK 5 - HER BURIED SECRET

BOOK 6 - HER WORST MISTAKE

Book 7 - Her Silent Misery

In The Summer Isle Series

It's paradise on the sparkling tropical shores of Hideaway Isle, Florida. But despite postcard-worthy appearances, there's trouble lurking just beyond the sun, sand, and sea that promises to wreak havoc in this seemingly idyllic utopia.

With riveting turns that will leave you breathless, each Summer Isle novel features a deep dive into a different islander's story.

Short Story Prequel - The Boy on Sunset and Main

Download it Free at Kelly's website: kellyutt.com

Book 1 - The Sisters of Kestrel Cay

Book 2 - The Girl in Hideaway Park

Book 3 - The Man at Nimbus Marina

In The Past Life Series

The Past Life Series chronicles the Hartmann and Davies families across time and space. This life-affirming story, anchored by the deep affection between George and Alessandra, reveals how the connections we share can ground us during even the most difficult times as we endeavor to learn what we're made of.

Join the family you'll feel like you already know as, together, they explore the meaning of life beyond what lies on the surface and fight to keep each other safe.

Short Story Prequel - Wait For Our Turn

Download it Free at Kelly's website: kellyutt.com

Book 1 - Tell Me I'm Safe

Book 2 - Show Me the Danger

Book 3 - Keep Them From Harm

Book 4 - Take Me to Fight

Book 5 - Pick Up the Pieces

————

Be the first to know when new books are released by signing up for Kelly's e-mail list at www.kellyutt.com.

Kindle Unlimited Subscribers read for free.

ABOUT THE AUTHOR

STANDARDS OF STARLIGHT BOOKS
KELLY UTT

Kelly Utt writes emotional novels for readers who enjoy both suspense and sentimentality. She was born in Youngstown, Ohio in 1976.

Kelly grew up with a dad who would read a book on a weighty topic, ask her to read it, too, and then insist they discuss it together, igniting her passion for life's big questions. That passion is often reflected inKelly's novels, giving them a depth which leaves readers wanting more and thinking about her stories long after the last lines are read.

She holds a Bachelor's degree in psychology from the

University of Tennessee, Knoxville and she studied graduate-level interactive media at Quinnipiac University.

Kelly lives in the Nashville suburb of Franklin, Tennessee with her husband and sons.

www.kellyutt.com

www.ingramcontent.com/pod-product-compliance
Lightning Source LLC
Chambersburg PA
CBHW071300190726
48292CB00007B/2618